*Two Days
of the Terrestrial Globe*

and Other Stories

Two Days in the Life of the Terrestrial Globe
and Other Stories

Vladimir Odoevsky

Translated by Neil Cornwell

ONEWORLD
CLASSICS

ONEWORLD CLASSICS LTD
London House
243-253 Lower Mortlake Road
Richmond
Surrey TW9 2LL
United Kingdom
www.oneworldclassics.com

These translations of 'Two Days in the Life of the Terrestrial Globe' and
'The Witness' first published in English in *Odoevsky's Four Pathways
into Modern Fiction* by Manchester University Press, 2010. All other
translations first published by Oneworld Classics Ltd in 2012.

Translation and notes © Neil Cornwell, 2012
Cover image © Sam Haque (sam.haque@me.com)

Printed and bound by CPI Group (UK) Ltd, Croydon, CR0 4YY

ISBN: 978-0-7145-4388-8

Contents

INTRODUCTION

Vladimir (or V.F.) Odoevsky (1804–69) was the last member of a princely Russian family that traced its descent from Rurik (the Viking leader who founded Russia in the ninth century). Odoevsky is now mainly remembered as one of the best Russian Romantic storytellers, specialising in the Gothic fantastic, as well as a significant author in the emerging genre of the (pre-Tolstoyan) society tale and, by no means least, of the unusual philosophical frame-tale novel, *Russian Nights* (1844).

Odoevsky was, though, a man of many parts, talents and careers. He held various posts in government service in St Petersburg, and finally returned to his native Moscow in the 1860s as a senator. But he was also a musical expert (critic, musicologist and minor composer – even inventing his own instrument) and a keen writer of educational works for the peasantry (before Leo Tolstoy embarked upon this). In addition, he was an amateur scientist, directed a major library and a museum, and spent much of his mid-life on philanthropic work. He even wrote cookery articles, under the name "Mister Puff". He knew all the big cultural figures: in literary life from Pushkin, Gogol and the young Dostoevsky to Tolstoy; and in musical life from Glinka to the young Tchaikovsky. Despite his aristocratic lineage (as a "Prince", or *Kniaz'*), he depended throughout on his government salary and publishing royalties for a living. A range of commentators, from various epochs, have dubbed him "the Russian Hoffmann", "the philosopher-prince", "a Russian Faust" and even "the Russian Goethe".

After his death, comparatively little attention was paid to Odoevsky's life and work until the republications and reassessments of the twentieth century. The main exception to this situation, even throughout the anti-Romanticism rigours of much of the Soviet period, was his unfailing popularity as an author of children's stories.

From being something of an "angry young man" of Russian literature in the early 1820s, Odoevsky progressed through his flourishing literary period as a leading Romantic writer of mystical and Gothic leanings, before maturing, having collected his three volumes of *Works* in 1844, into an over-conscientious public servant and an indefatigable philanthropist. Much later attempts to return to literature added little of any real significance to his oeuvre.

Of the eight works selected for presentation (ordered according to the dates of their original publication) in the present volume, at least half are translated into English for the first time. The 'Beethoven' and 'Piranesi' stories, translated by others back in the 1960s for the complete edition in English of *Russian Nights*, are here offered in re-translated versions. These eight works may also be seen as illustrating quite a number of the main aspects characterising Odoevsky's fiction.

'Two Days in the Life of the Terrestrial Globe' is a short work in the then newly emerging realm of Russian science fiction (written as early as 1825). The Comet Biela, on the approach of which this story is based, was a feared space object of the time, which had been calculated to collide with the Earth in the year 4339 (hence too Odoevsky's subsequent unfinished novella, *The Year 4338*, published in its fullest version only in 1926). In fact that comet burnt up later in the nineteenth century.

'Beethoven's Last Quartet' represents Odoevsky's penchant for the artistic, or indeed the musical story: *Russian Nights* also includes the fascinating and considerably longer "biographical" tale 'Sebastian Bach'. The Beethoven story should, ostensibly, refer to the composer's final string quartet, Opus 135; however, it is more than tempting to connect it to the harshly difficult and advanced *Grosse Fuge* (Opus 133), originally written as the finale to the Opus 130 quartet (No. 13, in B flat major). While the story is of course fictional and Romantic in approach, the reference to musicians throwing down their bows in desperation has an apparent basis in fact – at least as reported in rehearsals taking place in Russia in the late 1820s.

'Opere del Cavaliere Giambattista Piranesi' (or 'The Works of Piranesi'), like the Beethoven tale, was first published as a separate story, and later revised and subsumed into *Russian Nights*. Again this is an artistic (this time rather an architectural) tale, with a Neapolitan setting, and with it come the motifs of fantasy and supplanted, or adopted, biography (which may well have been inspired by Hoffmann's tale 'Ritter Gluck').

'The Little Town in the Snuffbox' remains probably the most popular of Odoevsky's magical children's stories (written under the pen name of "Granddad Irinei"). 'The Black Glove' is a society tale, notable for its highly satirical treatment of the supposed introduction of aspects of English (though partly as well Scottish) thought and attitudes into Russian society. 'The Apparition' here represents Odoevsky's Gothic-fantastic tendency, if only, in this particular instance, as a satirical play on the genre of the ghost story. 'The Witness' brings together a monk and the motifs of the duel and confession, in a manner strongly anticipatory of a striking episode to come much later in the biography of Father Zosima, in Dostoevsky's *The Karamazov Brothers*. Finally, in 'Imbroglio', Odoevsky returns to an Italian (and again largely Neapolitan) setting, to offer his readers an involved and unwittingly adventurous traveller's tale.

Two Days in the Life
of the Terrestrial Globe

and Other Stories

TWO DAYS IN THE LIFE
OF THE TERRESTRIAL GLOBE

1828; dated 1825

T HERE WERE A LOT OF GUESTS at Countess B—'s. It was midnight, the candles were getting used up, and the conversational heat was weakening, along with the decreasing light. Already, young girls were starting to talk over all the costumes for the next ball, the men had finished telling each other all the city news, the younger ladies had picked over all their acquaintances one by one, and the older ones had predicted the fates of several marriages. The gamblers had settled up amongst themselves and, having rejoined the social circle, had livened it up quite a bit with their tales of the mockery of fate, causing quite a few smiles and quite a few sighs, but soon this subject too had been exhausted. The hostess, who was extremely well versed in high-society chatter, any lull in which would be understood as boredom, was using all her skills to stir up garrulity in her tired guests. But all her efforts would have been in vain, had she not happened to glance out of the window. By good fortune, the comet was just then roaming over the starry sky and impelling astronomers to calculate, journalists to pontificate, simple folk to predict, and just about everyone else to have something to say about it. However, not one person from this entire company of gentry was as committed to it at this moment in time as Countess B—. In one instant, coming to the Countess's rescue, the comet had jumped from the horizon right into her drawing room, and had forced its way through an unbelievable quantity of hats and bonnets,

3

to be greeted by a similarly immeasurable quantity of different comments, some humorous and some regrettable. Some people were indeed afraid that this comet would play tricks on them; others, laughing, were convinced that it augured some wedding, or some divorce, and so on and so forth.

"You must be joking," said one of the guests, who had spent his whole life in society, engaged in astronomy (*par originalité*). "You may joke, but I remember one astronomer declaring that comets can come very close to the Earth, even collide with it – and then it would be no joke at all."

"Oh! How terrible!" the ladies cried. "But tell us, what would happen then, when a comet hits the Earth? Will the Earth fall down?" several voices muttered.

"The Earth will be shattered to bits," said the society astronomer.

"Oh, my God! And so that's when the social world will really be seen for what it is," said one rather aged lady.

"Rest assured," replied the astronomer, "other scientists maintain that this cannot happen, and that the Earth gets one degree nearer to the Sun every hundred and fifty years and that the day will finally come when the Earth will get burned up by the Sun."

"Oh, stop, do stop," cried the ladies. "How awful!"

The astronomer's words attracted widespread attention; at this point, endless arguments began. There were no disasters, at that moment, to which the terrestrial globe was not being subjected. They were burning it in fire, drowning it in water, and all of this was being affirmed, of course, not through the testimony of any scientists, but by quoting the utterances of some dear deceased uncle, who had been a chamberlain, or some late aunt, who had been a lady of state, and so on.

"Listen," the hostess finally exclaimed, "instead of arguing about it, let's, every one of us, write down on a piece of paper our thoughts on the subject, and then, why don't we all guess who wrote down this or that opinion?"

"Oh, yes! Yes, let's all write something," all the guests shouted…

"How do you want us to write it?" asked one young man timidly. "In French or in Russian?"

"*Fi donc – mauvais genre!*" said the hostess. "Who in this day and age writes in French? *Messieurs et Mesdames!* You have to write in Russian."

Paper was given out. Many sat down there and then at the table, but a lot of people, realising that things were stretching to an inkwell and to the Russian language, whispered into their neighbours' ear that there were still a number of visits to be made – and promptly disappeared.

When the writing had been finished, all the bits of paper were mixed up, and each person in turn read out their allotted piece. What follows is one of these conjectures, which seemed to us more remarkable than the rest, and which we here impart to our readers.

I

It had come about. The destruction of the terrestrial globe had begun. The astronomers have pronounced; the people's voice corroborates their view. This voice is implacable; it faithfully fulfils its promises. This comet, unprecedented until now, at an immeasurable speed accelerates towards the Earth. The sun only has to go down for this dreadful *wayfarer* to flare up. Delights are forgotten, misfortunes are forgotten, passions are stilled, desires have faded; there is neither peace nor activity, neither sleep nor wakefulness. Both day and night, people of all callings, in all conditions, lament upon the squares, and their trembling, pale faces are illuminated by a crimson flame.

Huge towers were turned into an observatory. Day and night the gazes of astronomers were fixed on the sky. Everyone came running to them, as though to all-powerful gods. Their words went flying from mouth to mouth. Astronomy was turning into the popular science. Everyone was doing calculations of the size of the comet and the speed of its motion. They were thirsting for mistakes in the astronomers' computations, but didn't find them.

"Look here, just look," one person said, "yesterday it was no bigger than the Moon, but now it's twice the size... What's it going to be like tomorrow?"

"Tomorrow it'll run into the Earth and crush us," said another...

"Couldn't we go off to the other side of the globe?" said a third person.

"Couldn't we construct defensive positions to repulse it with machines?" said a fourth. "What is the government thinking about?"

"There's no way out!" shouted one young man, out of puff. "I've just come from the tower – the scientists are saying that, even before it runs into the Earth, there will be storms, earthquakes and the surface will be ablaze..."

"Who will stand against the anger of God?" exclaimed one elder.

Meanwhile time moves on and with it grow the size of the comet and public alarm as well. It is now getting visibly bigger. By day, the sun shuts it out; at night it hangs over the Earth as a fiery cleft. Already a silent, awesome certainty had given way to despair. Neither groan nor lamentation was to be heard. The prisons were opened: the freed prisoners wander among the crowds with drooping heads. Rarely, only rarely, are the silence and the inaction interrupted: there's the cry of an infant who has been left without food, but then he will be silent again, admiring the awful heavenly spectacle; or now a father embraces the killer of his son.

But when the wind blows or thunder resounds, the crowd will start to stir – and everyone's lips are ready to mouth the question, but they fear to utter it.

In a secluded street of one European city an eighty-year-old man at his domestic hearth was cooking himself some food: suddenly his son runs up to him.

"What are you doing, Father?" he exclaims.

"What should I be doing?" the old man replies calmly. "You've all left – you're running about the streets, whereas I just go hungry…"

"Father! Is it really the time now to be thinking about food?"

"It's precisely this time, as it always is…"

"But our destruction…"

"Calm down. This groundless fear will pass, as do all earthly calamities…"

" But have you really completely lost your hearing and your vision?"

"Quite the opposite; not only have I preserved both, but also something above that, which you don't have: peace of spirit and strength of reason. Calm down, I say to you. The comet just appeared unexpectedly and will disappear likewise; and the destruction of the Earth is not at all as imminent as you think. The Earth has still not achieved maturity… an inner feeling assures me of that…"

"My dear Father! Your whole life you've had a stronger belief in this feeling, or in your daydreams, than in reality! Are you really, even now, going to remain dedicated to imagination?"

"The fear that I can see on your face, and the faces of those like you! This shabby fear is not compatible with the profound moment of demise…"

"How dreadful!" exclaimed the young man. "My father has completely lost his reason…"

At that same instant a terrible thunderbolt shook the territory, lightning flared, rain deluged down, a gale removed roofs from the buildings – the population threw themselves to the ground…

The night passed, the sky brightened and a gentle zephyr dried the ground, which had been awash with rain… The people did not dare to raise their lowered heads; eventually they did take the liberty. They by now feel themselves to be in the guise of bodiless spirits... Finally they stand up and look about them: the same familiar places, the same bright sky, the same people. An involuntary motion lifts everyone's gaze to the sky: the comet was moving away from the skyline.

II

This brought on a collective feast of the terrestrial globe. There was no tempestuous joy at this feast; nor were loud ejaculations heard! Long since had lively merriment turned for them into silent delight, into the usual round. Long since had they stepped over the obstacles preventing a human being from being a human being. The memory had already gone of the times when crude matter could laugh at the efforts of the spirit, when need gave way to necessity. The times of imperfection and prejudice had long since passed, together with human diseases. The planet was the mighty dwelling place of only the most powerful tsars, so no one was surprised at nature's magnificent feast. Everyone awaited it, for long had the premonition of it appeared to the imagination of the chosen ones in the form of a delightful vision. No one asked others anything about it; a triumphant thought shone across all faces and everyone could understand this mute eloquence. Quietly, the Earth drew near to the Sun, and an unburning warmth, like a fire of inspiration, extended across it. Just another moment – and the heavenly became the earthly, the earthly the heavenly: the Sun became the Earth and the Earth the Sun...

BEETHOVEN'S LAST QUARTET

1830 / 1844

I had not the slightest hesitation in supposing that Krespel had
gone mad, but the Professor was of the contrary opinion. "There
are men," he said, "whom Nature, or some peculiar destiny has
robbed of that outer covering beneath which we others conceal
the madness within us. They are like insects with thin integu-
ments, whose visible play of muscles seems a deformity, though
in reality it is the perfectly normal thing. What in us remains as
thought, in Krespel's case is translated into action."

*Hoffmann**

I T WAS THE YEAR 1827, in spring; in one of the houses on
the Viennese outskirts, a few lovers of music were performing a new quartet by Beethoven, which was hot off the press.
With amazement and vexation they were following through the
outrageous lurches of this genius in decline: there was such a
change in his writing! The charms of original melody, filled
with poetic thought, had disappeared; the exquisite finish had
been transformed into the laborious pedantry of an untalented
counterpointist; the fire that had previously flamed in his fast
allegros and, gradually strengthening, had overflowed like
boiling lava in full, huge consonances, had collapsed amid
incomprehensible dissonance; and the original, light-hearted
themes of the jolly minuets had been transformed into gallops
and warbles, impossible on any instrument. Everywhere there
were primitive, unattainable strivings towards effects that have
no place in music; everywhere there was some dark feeling,
not even making any sense to itself. And yet this was the same
Beethoven, the very one whose name, along with those of

9

Haydn and Mozart, is uttered with such Teutonic pride and joy! Several times, driven to despair by the incomprehensibility of the composition, the musicians threw down their bows and were ready to ask: was this not a mockery of the works of an immortal? Some attributed this degeneration to the deafness which had stricken Beethoven over the last years of his life; others leant rather towards the insanity which had at times also blackened his creative gift. Here an expression of insincere sympathy escaped; and there some other wag recalled how Beethoven, at a concert where his last symphony was being played, waved his arms about, completely out of time, thinking he was conducting the orchestra – oblivious to the real *Kapellmeister* standing behind him. But they soon took up their bows again and, out of respect for the former reputation of the famous symphonist, and as though even against their will, carried on playing away at his unintelligible composition.

Suddenly the door opened and a man walked in, wearing a black frock coat, without a tie, and with dishevelled hair; his eyes were burning – but this was not the fire of giftedness. Only the beetling brow, the harshly clipped extremities of the forehead, indicated the unusual development of the type of musical organ that had so taken Hall's fancy* when he had examined the head of Mozart.

"Excuse me, gentlemen," said the unexpected visitor, "permit me to look round your apartment – it's being offered for rent..."

Then he placed his hands behind his back and approached the players. The gathering respectfully yielded a place to him. He leant his head first to one side and then to the other, trying hard to listen to the music, but to no avail: a hail of tears started to fall from his eyes. He silently moved away from the performers and sat down in a further corner of the room, with his face covered in his hands. But hardly had the bow of the first violinist begun to squeal up by the bridge on an unexpected note added to a *septième* chord, and a wild consonance had resounded in the doubled notes of the other instruments, than the afflicted visitor jumped out of his skin, shouting: "I can hear! I can hear!" In tempestuous joy, he started clapping his hands and stamping his feet.

"Ludwig!" said the young girl who had come in after him, "Ludwig! It's time to go home. We are only in the way here!"

He looked at the girl, knew what she meant, and without saying a word plodded after her, like a child.

At the edge of the city, on the third floor of an old stone house, there is a small, stuffy room divided by a partition. A bed with a torn blanket, a few reams of music paper, and the remnants of a fortepiano – these comprised the only decoration. This was the domain, this was the world of the immortal Beethoven. For the whole way, he did not say a word; but when they got there Ludwig sat down on the bed, took the girl's hand and said to her:

"My dear Louisa! You are the only one who understands me; you are the only one who is not afraid of me; you're the only one I don't embarrass... You may think that all these gentlemen who perform my music understand me: that's never been the case! Not one of these gentlemen-*Kapellmeisters* around is even capable of conducting it; they only care about the orchestra playing in time, and as for the music – what's that to them! They think that I am going downhill; I even noticed that some of them seemed to be sniggering as they were playing my quartet – and that's a real sign that they have never understood me. On the contrary: only now have I become a truly great musician. Walking home, I thought up a symphony that will make my name live forever; I'll write it out and burn all the old ones. In it I am going to overturn all the laws of harmony, I'm going to discover effects that no one has even suspected until now; I'll construct it on a chromatic melody with twenty kettledrums; I'll bring into it chords from a hundred bells, tuned against a range of tuning forks. For..." – he added in a whisper – "I'll let you into a secret: when you took me to the

11

bell-tower, I discovered that bells are the most harmonious instrument, which can be used perfectly in a quiet adagio. I'll bring drumbeats and gunshots into the finale – and I shall hear this symphony, Louisa!" – he exclaimed, beside himself in delight – "I hope I shall hear it," he added smilingly, after a short reflection. "Do you remember that time in Vienna, in the presence of the crowned heads of the whole world, I conducted the orchestra in my *Battle of Waterloo*?* Thousands of musicians, submissive to my gesticulation, twelve *Kapellmeisters*, and the fire of battle and cannon all around… Oh!… to this day that's my best work, never mind what that pedant Weber says!* – But what I am going to write now will eclipse even that composition. I can't stop myself from giving you some conception of it."

With these words Beethoven went over to the fortepiano, on which there remained not a single entire string, and with an air of importance pounded at the soundless keys. Monotonously they thudded against the dried-up wood of the ruined instrument, and at the same time the most complex fugues in five and six voices overran all the mysteries of counterpoint, of their own accord capitulating to the fingers of the creator of the incidental music to *Egmont*; and he was striving to impart the maximum expression to his music… But suddenly he struck the keys hard with the flat of his hand and stopped.

"Do you hear it?" he asked Louisa. "This is a chord which no one until now has dared to use. There it is! I'm going to combine all the tones of the chromatic scale into one concord and I'll prove to the pedants that this chord is right. – But I can't hear it, Louisa, I can't hear it! Can you understand what it means not to hear one's own music? All the same, it seems to me that, when I collect wild sounds into one concord – then it's just as though it is ringing in my ear. And the more depressed I get, Louisa, the more notes I feel like adding to this *septième* chord, the true qualities of which no one before me has understood… But that's enough! Perhaps I have worn you out with it, like I wear everyone out these days? – Only, do you know what? For such wonderful inventiveness, I can reward myself today with a glass of wine. What do you think of that, Louisa?"

Tears welled up in the eyes of the poor girl, who alone of all the pupils of Beethoven, did not abandon him and, under the pretence of taking lessons, supported him by her own labours. She supplemented by these means the miserable revenue that Beethoven received for his compositions, the greater part of which was expended pointlessly in incessant changes of accommodation, and the distribution of largesse to all and sundry. There was no wine! There scarcely remained a few *groschen* for bread… But she soon turned away from Ludwig, in order to cover her embarrassment, poured some water into a glass – and presented it to Beethoven.

"A splendid Rhine wine!" he said, taking gradual sips with the appearance of an expert. – "A royal Rhine wine! As though from the cellar of my father – Friedrich of blessed memory.* I remember this wine really well! It gets better by the day – that's the sign of a good wine!" And with these words, in a raucous but certain voice, he began singing his music to the famous song of Goethe's Mephistopheles:

Es war einmal ein König
Der hatt' einen grossen Floh*

But, despite himself, he frequently combined it with the mysterious melody by means of which Beethoven had defined Mignon.*

"Listen, Louisa," he said finally, giving the glass back to her, "the wine has bucked me up, and I intend telling you something which I've been both wanting and not wanting to tell you now, for a long time. Do you know, I think I'm not going to live for very much longer – and what sort of a life do I have, anyway? – it's a chain of endless tribulations. From my most youthful days, I caught sight of the abyss which is the division between thought and expression. Alas, never have I been able to give full expression to my soul; never have I been able to transfer onto paper what my imagination has unveiled. I write; they play it – but it's not the same!... It's not only that it is not what I had felt; it was never even the same thing I had written. A melody would get lost because some mediocre craftsman had not thought of putting in an extra valve; some awful bassoonist would make me rework an entire symphony just because his bassoon wouldn't produce a couple of bass notes; or a violinist would diminish an essential sound in a chord because he found it difficult to deal with double-stopping. And as for voices, and the singing, and oratorio and opera rehearsals... Oh, the hell of it haunts my ear to this day! But I was still happy then. Sometimes I would notice some inkling of inspiration come over these inane performers; I would catch in the sounds they made something resembling the dark notion embedded in my imagination; then I would be beside myself, vanishing into the harmony created by me. But there came a time when, little by little, my keen ear began to coarsen: it still retained sufficient sensitivity to catch the mistakes of musicians, but it shut itself to beauty; a cloud of gloom gripped it – and I cannot hear my compositions any more, I can't hear, Louisa!... Entire ranges of harmonic concords drift about in my imagination; original melodies cut one across the other, merging into a mysterious unity. I want to express it – but it has all disappeared: obstinate material-ity will not produce for me a single sound – rough feelings obliterate the soul's entire vibrancy. Oh, what can be more terrible than this discord between soul and feelings, between soul and soul! To engender in the mind one's creative work and by the hour to be dying in the pangs of parturition!... The death of the soul! How terrible, how alive this death is!

"And what's more, this senseless Gottfried drives me into pointless musical argumentation, forcing me to explain why in one place or another I employed such-and-such a fusion of motifs, or such-and-such a combination of instruments, when I cannot really explain this to myself! As though such people would know what a musician's soul is, what a human soul is! They think it can be etched by the fabrications of craftsmen working on their instruments, going by the rules which the dried-up brain of some theoretician thinks up in his spare time... No, when this moment of rapture comes over me, that's when I convince myself that such a perverse state in art cannot continue; that the dilapidated forms will be replaced by new, fresh ones; that all of our present instruments will be left behind, and their places taken by other ones, which will perform the works of geniuses to perfection; and that the absurd gulf between written and played music will finally disappear.

"I have spoken about this to our professorial gentlemen, but they didn't understand me, just as they didn't understand the power inherent in artistic rapture, and just as they didn't understand that I am admonishing time and operating in accordance with the inner laws of nature that have yet to come to the notice of the common herd and which are, at other times, incomprehensible even to me... Fools! In their frigid delectation, when they've nothing better to do, they will pick out a theme, they arrange it, they extend it and they won't fail then to repeat it in another key. Then, as if to order, they add in the wind instruments or some quaint chord on which they ruminate over and again, and all this they will smooth out and lick clean so prudently. What do they expect? I can't work like that... They compare me to Michelangelo, but how did the creator of *Moses* work? In anger, and in rage, with fierce blows of the hammer, he struck away at the inanimate marble and forced it to produce the vibrant thought lying hidden beneath the shell of stone. That's me, too! I don't comprehend frigid delectation! What I understand is that rapture, when, for me, the whole world is transformed into

15

harmony: every kind of feeling, every kind of thought sounds in me, all the forces of nature become my weapons, my blood boils in my veins, a shudder passes through my body and the hair on my head is aroused... And it's all in vain! Yes, what is it all for? What's the point? You're alive, you're tormented, you're thinking; you've written it down, and that's that! Creation's sweetest pangs are riveted to the paper – you can't bring them back! The ideas of a proud creative spirit are consigned demeaningly to the dungeon; the lofty exertion of the terrestrial creator, who has challenged the very power of nature to a debate, becomes mere matter in human hands! And people? People! They come along, they listen, they pass judgement – as though they were actually judges, as though your creations were for them! What is it to them if a notion that has taken on an image they can understand happens to be a link in an endless chain of notions and sufferings? That the instant when an artist comes down to a human level is just a fragment from a lengthy and morbid life of immeasurable emotion? That his every expression, his every written line, was born from the bitter tears of some seraph riveted to human clothing, and ready to give up half a lifetime, just to inhale for a minute the fresh air of inspiration? And meanwhile the time is approaching – just like it did just now – when you feel that your soul has burned out, your powers are weakening, your head is sore: whatever you may be thinking, everything is getting muddled up and everything is obscured by some sort of screen... Oh! Louisa, how I would like to convey my last thoughts and feelings to you, those which are preserved still in the treasure-house of my soul – so that they don't vanish for ever... But what is that I hear?"

With these words, Beethoven leapt up and with a strong blow of the hand flung open the window, through which, from a nearby house, harmonious sounds were wafting in...

"I can hear!" exclaimed Beethoven, throwing himself onto his knees and emotionally extending his hands towards the open window. "It's the *Egmont* music – that's what it is. Yes, I recognize it: we have the wild cries of battle; and now the storm of passions. It flares up and rages; there it is now at its height – but now it's all died down, and there's just an icon-lamp left, which is going out, it's being extinguished – but not for all eternity... Again the trumpets have sounded: the whole world is being filled with them, and no one can stifle them..."

* * *

At the sumptuous ball given by one of the Viennese ministers, crowds of people were gathering and dispersing.

"What a shame!" someone said, "The theatrical *Kapellmeister* Beethoven has died, and they say he left nothing to cover his burial."

But this voice was soon lost in the crowd: everyone was paying attention to the words of the two diplomats who were talking about some argument which had taken place between whomever it was, at some German prince or other's palace.

B EFORE WE DEPARTED we went to bid farewell to one of
our relatives, who was getting on in years, rather staid,
and respected all round. He had throughout his life only one
passion, of which his late wife would say, in these words: "So,
to give you an example, Alexei Stepanych: there's no better
man, husband or father, or master – everything would be fine,
if it were not for this one unhappy weakness..."

At this point our old aunt would come to a stop. Any stranger
would often ask: "What is it, not heavy drinking, dear lady?"
– and would get ready to propose some medicinal cure. But it
would ensue that this weakness was merely *bibliomania*. It's
true that this passion in our uncle was a very strong one, but
it was, seemingly, the only tiny window through which his soul
could peep into the poetical world. In all other respects, the old
chap was just like any other uncle – he smoked, he would play
whist for days on end, and abandoned himself with delectation
to our northern trait of indifference. But once things got to
books, the old chap would be quite regenerated. When he found
out the reason for our journey, he gave a broad smile and said:

"Youthfulness, youthfulness! Romanticism, that's all it is!
Why don't you take stock all around you? I can assure you
that, without travelling far away, you would come across quite
enough material."

"We are not averse to that," replied one of us. "When we
have managed to take a look at those different ones, then,

quite possibly, we'll get back to our own home place. But, to begin with, looking at the materials of others seems the proper way to go about it. And beyond that, the people whom we are thinking of belong to all nations at once, while many are either just living, or have not yet quite died: it may well be that their relatives will take offence... Far be it from us to imitate those gents who bake themselves alive for their own glorification, and for that of their friends, in the utter certainty that upon their death no one will bother doing it."

"That's true, that's true!" replied the old man. "Oh, these relations! In the first place, you don't get anywhere with them, and secondly, to them a remarkable person is nothing more than an uncle, a dear old cousin, and suchlike and so forth. Off you go, young fellows, and take in the world: it's a healthy thing for body and soul. I myself, in my young days, travelled overseas seeking out rare books that could have been bought here at half the price. And as for bibliography. Don't go thinking that all there is to it is just rosters of books and bindings; it can sometimes provide you with completely unexpected delights. Do you want me to tell you all about my meeting with one person of your type? Just see if he doesn't find his way into chapter one of your travel notes!"

We indicated our willingness, just as recommended now to our readers, and the old chap just carried on:

"You, perhaps, might have seen that caricature, which depicts a scene in Naples. Out in the open air, under a tattered awning, there is a bookstall. Piles of old books and old prints. There's a Madonna up above. Mount Vesuvius is in the distance. In front of the little shop is a Capuchin monk and a young chap in a big straw hat, from whose pocket a little *lazzarone** is deftly pulling out a handkerchief. I don't know how the blasted painter managed to catch hold of this scene, except that this young man is actually me! I recognize my caftan and my straw hat. I did have my handkerchief stolen that day, and even on my face there must have been the same daft expression.

"The point is that I didn't have much money then – far from sufficient to satisfy my passion for antiquarian books. What is more, I, like all bibliophiles, was mean to an extreme. This factor compelled me to pass over public auctions, at which, like in a game of cards, a fervid bibliophile may completely ruin himself. But, there again, I zealously visited a small shop in which I spent little enough but, on the other hand, took the pleasure of foraging through everything from top to bottom.

"You, perhaps, have really felt all the joys of bibliomania: it is one of the very strongest passions, when you give it free rein; and I can totally understand that German pastor, whom bibliomania reduced to committing murder. I myself, not long ago at all – although old age destroys all the passions, even bibliomania – was ready to kill one friend of mine, who absolutely dispassionately, as though in a public library, cut out the only leaf in my Elzevir* which proved that the copy had full margins.* And he, that vandal, even showed surprise at my annoyance.

"Even now I haven't stopped visiting the dealers. I know by heart all their warped notions, their prejudices and ruses, and even now I count these minutes as, if not the happiest, then at least the most pleasurable in my life. You go in: at once the cordial proprietor removes his hat, and with full mercantile generosity, proposes the novels of Genlis,* and last year's almanacs, along with *Animal Medical Care*. But you only need to utter a single word and that will straight away curb his tiresome enthusiasm. Just ask him – 'And where are the medical books?' – and the proprietor will put his hat back on, he'll show you a corner covered in dust and full of books with parchment binding, and then calmly settle down again to finish reading the previous month's academic gazette.

"Here I should bring to your notice, young fellows, that still, in many of our bookshops, any book having a parchment

binding and a Latin title is entitled to be termed medical. And
so you can judge for yourselves what latitude there is for a bibliophile. Amid *The Science of Women's Business, in Five Parts,
Furnished with Illustrations* by Nestor Maximovich Ambodik,*
and the *Bonati Thesaurus medico-practicus undique collectus*,*
there will suddenly appear a little pamphlet that's tattered,
dirtied and covered with dust. You take a look, and it's *Advis
fidelle aux véritables Hollandais touchant ce qui s'est passé
dans les villages de Bodegrave et Swammerdam*,* 1673 – how
fascinating! But it seems to be an Elzevir! – a name which brings
into a sweet tremble a bibliophile's entire nervous system... You
throw aside a few yellowed copies of *Hortus sanitatis, Jardin
de dévotion*, or *Les Fleurs de bien dire, recueillies aux cabinets
des plus rares esprits pour exprimer les passions amoureuses de
l'un et de l'autre sexe par forme de dictionnaire** – and there
appears before you a Latin booklet with no binding and no
beginning. You open it up: it seems like Virgil – but there's a
mistake in nearly every word!... Can it actually be? Aren't you
being carried away by a dream? Is it really the renowned edition of 1514, *Virgilius ex recensione Naugerii*?* And you don't
deserve to call yourself a bibliophile if your heart doesn't take
a jump from joy when, getting to the end, you catch sight of
four full pages of errata – a certain intimation that this exactly
is that most rare and precious Aldine edition,* the pearl of all
libraries, most of the copies of which the publisher himself
destroyed in anger at the misprints.

"In Naples I found few opportunities for the satisfaction of
my passion, and so you can imagine with what amazement,
strolling through the Piazza Nova, I spotted piles of parch-
ments. This was the exact instant of bibliomanic stupefac-
tion that was caught by my uninvited portrait-painter... In
any event, I, with all the guile of a bibliophile, nonchalantly
came up to the bookstall and, flicking through ancient prayer
books with a concealed impatience, at first failed to notice
that a figure in an old-fashioned French caftan, a powdered

wig and a carefully wound dangling bun, had gone up to an enormous folio in the other corner. I don't know what prompted us both to turn round, but in this figure I recognized the crank who, always in the same rig-out, strolled pompously around Naples and at every meeting, especially with the ladies, with a smile would raise his worn-out boat-shaped hat. For some time already I had noted this eccentric and was highly delighted to have the opportunity of getting to meet him. I glanced at the book opened before him: it was a collection of some sort of badly reprinted architectural etchings. The eccentric was scrutinising them with great attention, measuring with his fingers the coloured columns, putting a finger to his forehead and getting absorbed into a deep meditation.

"'He's evidently an architect,' I thought: 'so, to be more appealing to him, I'll make out I'm a lover of architecture.' Just then my eyes lit on a collection of enormous folios on which was imprinted: *Opere del Cavaliere Giambatista Piranesi*. 'That's wonderful!' I thought. I took up one volume and opened it up. But the bygone projects in it of colossal buildings, the construction of which would take millions of people, millions of gold coins, and centuries – these cloven rocks taken up to mountain peaks, these rivers converted into fountains: all this so absorbed me, that for a minute I quite forgot my old crank. More than anything, I was staggered by one volume, filled almost from beginning to end with depictions of various sorts of prisons; endless vaults, bottomless caves, locks, chains, walls covered with growth and, for decoration, all the possible executions and tortures ever invented by man's criminal imagination... A coldness ran right through my veins and I unwittingly shut the book. At the same time, having noticed that the eccentric did not bestow upon my architectural enthusiasm the slightest attention, I decided to accost him with a question.

"'You are, of course, an enthusiast for architecture?' said I.

"'For architecture?' he repeated as though horror-struck. 'Yes,' he articulated, peering with a disdainful smile at my worn-out caftan, 'I am a great enthusiast for it!' and fell silent.

"'Is that all?' I thought. 'That's not saying very much.'

"'In that case,' I said, opening again one of the Piranesi volumes, 'you'd do better to have a look at these tremendous works of fantasy, rather than those cheaply printed pictures lying in front of you.'

"He came over to me reluctantly, with the air of a man annoyed that his business was being interfered with, but his glance had barely met the book open in front of me, before he sprang away from me in horror, and waved his hands, yelling: 'For God's sake, close it; close this good-for-nothing, dreadful book!'

"This seemed to me rather curious. 'I can only be taken aback at your repugnance for such a superb work. I am so keen on it that I shall purchase it straight away.' And upon these words, I pulled out my purse of money.

"'Money!' my crank muttered in the same resonant whisper of which I have been not long ago reminded by the one-and-only Karatygin in *The Life of a Gambler.** 'You have some money!' he repeated the word, his whole body trembling.

"I must admit, that this outburst from the architect rather dampened my eagerness to enter into a close friendship with him; but my curiosity overcame this.

"'Do you really need money?' I asked.

"'Me? I really do!' the architect muttered, 'and I've needed it for a very, very long time,' he added putting a stress on each word.

"'And is it very much that you need?' I asked with some sympathy. 'Maybe I would be able to help you.'

"'In the first place, I need just a pittance – a mere pittance, ten million gold coins.'

"'But why ever do you want so much?' I asked with some surprise.

"'So as to join up Etna and Vesuvius with a vault, for the triumphal gates and the beginning of the castle park which I've projected,' he replied, as though this were nothing unusual.

"I could hardly hold myself back from laughing.

"'Why, then,' I retorted, 'should you, a man with such colossal ideas, treat with such repulsion the plans of a designer who, in his own ideas, comes really quite close to you?'

"'Comes close?' exclaimed the recent arrival, ' – comes close! So why do you bother me about this accursed book, when I myself am the creator of it?'

"'No, that really is too much!' I replied. Uttering these words, I picked up the *Historical Dictionary* lying beside us and showed him the page on which was written: 'Giambattista Piranesi, the renowned architect... died in 1778...'

"'That's rubbish! It's a lie!' my architect shouted. 'Oh, I would be happy, were it the truth! But I live, to my own ruination, I still live – and this accursed book prevents me from dying.'

"My fascination increased with every passing moment.

"'Elucidate this aberration for me,' I said to him, 'entrust your woe to me: I say again, that perhaps I'll be able to help you.'

"The old fellow's face brightened up; he took me by the arm.

"'Here is not the place to talk about it. People who are in a position to do me harm could overhear us. Oh, I know these people... Come along with me; on the way, I'll tell you my terrible story.' So we went out.

"'And so, my good sir,' the old man resumed, 'you see in me the renowned and ill-starred Piranesi. I was born a man with talent – what am I saying? It's now too late to refuse to admit it – I was born with an exceptional genius. A passion for architecture developed in me from my childhood, and the great Michelangelo, who put up the Pantheon on the so-called huge church of St Peter in Rome – in his old age he was my teacher.* He got carried away by my plans and projects for buildings, and when I got to the age of twenty the great master released me, saying: "If you stay with me any longer, you will turn out only as my imitator; off you go, blaze a new trail, and you will immortalize your name without any efforts from me." I did as I was told, and from that moment my misfortunes began. I became short of money. I couldn't find work anywhere; unavailingly did I submit my projects to the Roman Emperor, and to the French King, and to popes and cardinals. They all heard me out, they all enthused, they all encouraged me, given that the passion for art, inflamed by my patron Michelangelo, still smouldered in Europe. They took care of me, as a man possessing the power to rivet unrenowned names to renowned monuments. But when things got to the point of construction, then they started putting things off for year after year. "When our finances improve; when our ships come home with overseas gold" – no go! I employed all my intrigues, every ingratiation unbecoming to a genius – and no-go! I myself took fright, seeing what degradation my lofty soul had to stoop to – and still no go! Nothing doing! Time passed, buildings got started and completed, my rivals gained their immortality, and I still roamed from court to court, from reception room to reception room, along with my portfolio, which to no purpose was getting more and more full with splendid and unrealizable projects. Shall I tell you how it felt, going into these rich halls with renewed hope in the heart, and coming out again in renewed despair? My prisons book represents within it only a hundredth part of what went on in my soul. In these dens my genius suffered; I champed on these chains, forgotten by an unthankful humanity... There was a hellish enjoyment in my invention of the torments engendered in my envenomed heart, in turning the sufferings of the spirit into sufferings of the body – but this was my sole delight, my sole relaxation.

"'Feeling the approach of old age, and reflecting that, even if anyone did desire to commission me for some construction or other, then I would not have sufficient life left in me for its completion – I decided to publish my projects, to show up my contemporaries, and so as to display to posterity the sort of man they had been unable to appreciate. I got down to this work with zeal, engraved day and night, and my projects made their way around the world, whether arousing laughter or surprise. But something entirely different started happening with me. Just listen, and be astonished... I had learned by now through bitter experience that every work coming from an artist's head gives birth to a torturer-spirit. Every building, every picture, every line formulated on canvas or paper serves as the abode for such a spirit. These spirits are the attributes of evil: they love to live, they love to multiply and to torment their creator for the cramped abode. No sooner had they scented out that their abode had to be confined just to engraved pictures, than they became incensed with me... I was on my deathbed already, when, all of a sudden... Have you heard of the man known as the Wandering Jew? Everything that is said about him is a lie: this ill-omened man is in front of you... I had scarcely begun to close my eyes in eternal sleep, when phantoms surrounded me in the guise of palaces, great chambers, houses, castles, vaults, columns. They all crushed me with their bulk, and with horrific laughter asked me for life. From that very minute, I have not known peace. The spirits generated by me persecute me: over there an almighty vault seizes me in its embrace; here towers are tearing after me, stepping it out in kilometres; over this way a window clanks in front of me with its enormous frames. Sometimes they shut me into my own dungeons, plunge me into bottomless wells, hammer me into my own chains, and spatter me with cold fungus from half-derelict vaults. They force me to go through all the torments invented by me: from the bonfire they throw me down on to the rack, from the rack on to a spit. Each nerve they expose to unexpected suffering; meanwhile they, the oppressors, spin about and guffaw at me, not letting me die, trying to elicit why

I have condemned them to a life that's not full and to eternal anguish. And then finally they throw the emaciated one, the enfeebled one, back down to earth.

"'Pointlessly I wander from country to country; pointlessly I look all round, as to whether some wonderful building somewhere, built by my rivals for a laugh on me, has not broken apart. Often, in Rome at night, I go up to the walls built by that lucky chap Michel and bash with my weak hand at this blasted cupola, which doesn't intend to stir. Or, in Pisa, I hang with both my arms onto this good-for-nothing tower, which for the duration of seven centuries has been slanting to the Earth but doesn't want ever to reach it. I've roamed right across Europe, Asia, Africa, and sailed across the sea; everywhere I look for ruined buildings which my creative might could reconstruct: I clap my hands at storms and earthquakes. Born with a poet's naked heart, I have felt deeply all that has been suffered by those unfortunates, deprived of their habitation through strikes from the horrors of nature. I wail along with those unlucky people, but I just have to tremble with joy at the sight of ruination... And all this is for nothing! My hour of creation has not yet begun, or it has already gone; much around me falls apart, but much still lives and prevents my thoughts from taking on life.

"'I know that my weakened eyelids will not close until my rescuer be found and all my colossal ideas be not merely on paper. But where is he? Where to find him? And even if I do find him, then my projects will already be antiquated; the age has already left much in them behind – and there is not the strength left to revitalize them!

"'Occasionally I can deceive my tormentors, persuading them that I am getting on with the bringing to fulfilment of one of my projects; and then for a bit they leave me in peace. That's just the situation I was in when I encountered you. But you took it into your head to open my accursed book in front of me. You didn't see it, but I... I could see clearly one of the temple pilasters, built in the mid-Mediterranean Sea starting to nod at me with its ragged head... Now you comprehend my misfortune: do help me, then, in accordance with your promise. Only ten million gold coins, I entreat you!' And with these words uttered, the poor devil fell to his knees in front of me.

"With amazement and compassion I looked upon the pauper, took out one gold coin, and said: 'Here you are, this is all that I can give you now.'

"The old fellow looked up at me despondently. 'That's what I foresaw,' he replied, 'but that, even, is fine: I'll put this money into the pot I'm assembling for the buying of Mont Blanc, to raze it completely. Or else it is going to block out the view from my amusement castle.'

"Upon these words, the old fellow hastily made off."

THE LITTLE TOWN IN THE SNUFFBOX

1834

for Oscar and Maisie Jones [translator's dedication]

PAPA PUT A SNUFFBOX down on the table.

"Come over here, Misha, and have a look at this," he said.

Misha was an obedient boy; he left his toys straight away and went over to Papa. And there certainly was something to look at! What a fine snuffbox it was – all different colours, out of tortoiseshell! And what there was on the lid! Gates, little turrets, a little house, another one, a third one, a fourth – you can't count them, each one smaller than the last one, and all of them golden; and the trees are also golden, and the little leaves on them are silver. And behind the trees a little sun is coming up, and pink rays are coming out from it, going all over the sky.

"What little town is that?" asked Misha.

"It's the little town of Ding-Ding," Papa replied and just touched the spring...

And what then? All of a sudden, you couldn't see where, music started playing. Misha couldn't make out where he heard this music coming from. He went over to the doors – wasn't it coming from the other room? And over to the clock – wasn't it in the clock? And over to the writing-desk, and over to the cabinet. He listened hard first in one place and then another; he even looked under the table... In the end Misha satisfied himself that the music was really playing in the snuffbox. He went over to it, and had a look. And from behind the trees the sun comes up, creeps quietly up into the sky, and the sky and

29

the little town get brighter and brighter; the little windows are burning with a clear light and from the turrets it's as though there's a radiance. And so the sun moved across the sky over to the other side, getting lower and lower, and finally disappeared completely behind a little hill; and the little town darkened, the shutters closed, and the turrets faded – only not for long. Now a star began to flicker, and then another, and now a horned moon looked out from behind the trees, and in the little town it got lighter again, the windows went silver, and from the turrets bluish rays reached out.

"Daddy! Daddy! Can't I go into this little town? How I'd really like to!"

"A bit difficult, my friend: this little town is not the right size for you."

"Never mind, Dad, I'm small enough. Just let me go there. I'd so like to find out what goes on in there…"

"Really, my dear chap, it's quite crowded enough in there, even without you."

"Oh, but who lives there, then?"

With these words, Papa lifted the lid on the snuffbox – and what did Misha see? He saw little bells, little hammers, a cylinder and wheels… Misha was really surprised.

"What are these little bells for? Why the hammers? What's the cylinder with the hooks for?" – Misha was asking his Papa.

And Papa replied: "I'm not going to tell you, Misha. You just have a closer look yourself, and think about it: maybe you'll even guess. Only don't touch this spring, otherwise the whole thing will break."

Papa went out of the room, and Misha stayed there, bending over the snuffbox. Now he sat there and sat there over it, looked and looked at it, thought and thought about it – how do the little bells ring?

Meanwhile, the music keeps playing and playing. But now it's getting quieter and quieter, as though something is clinging on to every note, as though something is pushing one sound away from another. So Misha looks at it: down at the bottom of the snuffbox a little door is opening, and from the door there runs out a little boy with a gold head, in a steel smock; he stops at the threshold and beckons Misha over.

"So why" – thought Misha – "did Daddy say that it's crowded enough in the little town, even without me? No, I can see that there are nice people living there, who are inviting me in to visit them."

"Only too pleased, with the greatest of pleasure!"

With these words, Misha ran over to the little door and to his surprise he found that the door turned out to be exactly the right size for him. Like a well-brought-up boy, he felt that, before anything else, he should say something to his companion.

"Would you mind telling me" – said Misha – "who it is I am speaking to?"

"Ding – ding – ding," replied the unknown boy, "I'm the little bell-boy, I live in this little town. We heard that you really wanted to come and visit us, and so we decided to ask you to be good enough to do us the honour. Ding – ding – ding, ding – ding – ding!"

Misha bowed to him very politely; the little bell-boy took him by the hand, and off they went. At this point Misha noticed that there was an arch above them, made out of multicoloured printed paper, with gold edging. In front of them was another arch, only a bit smaller; then a third one, smaller still; and a fourth, still smaller, and so on it went with all the other arches. The further away they were, the smaller they got, so that, with the last one, it looked as though his guide's head would hardly be able to go through it.

"I am very grateful to you for your invitation," Misha said to him, "but I don't know whether I'll really be able to take you up on it. It's true that I can walk through quite freely here, but down there, a bit further, look what low little arches you have – there I..., to be quite honest, down there I wouldn't be able to crawl through. I'd be surprised if you can get through under them."

"Ding – ding – ding!" the boy replied. "We'll get through, don't you worry, just follow me."

Misha did as he was told. And in actual fact, with every step they took, it seemed that the arches got a bit higher, and our boys managed to walk through everywhere, quite freely. When they had reached the last arch, then the little bell-boy asked Misha to look back. Misha turned to look, and what did he see? Now that first arch, the one he had gone up to walking through the little doors, looked so small to him – as though, while they had been walking, the arch had sunk lower. Misha was very surprised.

"What's the cause of that?" he asked his escort.

"Ding – ding – ding!" his escort replied, laughing. "That's the way it always seems from a distance. Obviously you've never paid much attention to anything in the distance. In the distance everything seems small, but as you go towards it, it gets bigger."

"Oh yes, that's true," replied Misha, "I didn't really think about that until now. And because of that, do you know what happened to me? The other day I wanted to do a drawing of Mamma playing the piano beside me, with Dad reading a book at the other end of the room. Only I couldn't manage to do this at all. I tried and tried, drawing it all as true to life as I could. But still, on my sheet of paper, Dad would come out sitting next to Mamma, with his armchair standing next to the piano, when I could see all too well that the piano was standing beside me, by the window, while Dad was sitting at the other end, by the fireplace. Mamma told me that I needed to draw Dad smaller, but I thought Mamma must be joking, because Dad is much taller than her. But now I see that she was telling the truth: Dad needed to be drawn small, because he was sitting a long way away. I'm very grateful for your explanation, very grateful."

The little bell-boy laughed for all he was worth: "Ding – ding – ding, that's really funny! Not to be able to draw your Papa and your Mamma! Ding – ding – ding, ding – ding – ding!"

"Can I just ask you: why do you keep saying 'ding – ding – ding' after every word?"

"Oh, it's just a saying we have," the little bell-boy replied.

"A saying?" remarked Misha. "Well, my Dad says it's really not at all good to get in the habit of repeating sayings."

The little bell-boy bit his tongue and didn't say another word.

Now there were more doors in front of them; they opened, and Misha found himself on the street. And what a street! What a little town it was! The roadway was paved with mother-of-pearl; the sky was all different colours, tortoiseshell; a golden sun was going across the sky; you just had to beckon to it, and it would come down from the sky, go right round your hand, and then go back up again. And the little houses were steel, polished, roofed with different coloured shells, and beneath every roof sat a little bell-boy with a little gold head, in a silver smock – and there were so many of them, and each one was smaller than the last one.

"No, now I'm not fooled any more," said Misha. "It just seems like that to me from a distance, but the little bells are really alike."

"Ah, but that's not right," replied his guide, "the little bells are not all alike. If they were really all the same, then we would all ring in the one tone, each one of us the same as the other. But you can hear the sort of tunes we turn out. That is because those of us who are a bit bigger have a voice that's a bit heavier. Don't you know that, really? So you see, Misha, let this be a lesson for you: from now on don't just laugh at anyone who uses a saying that you find odd; some people, even with this saying of theirs, might know more than you do, and you might learn something from them."

Now it was Misha's turn to bite his tongue.

Meanwhile they were surrounded by little bell-boys, who tugged at Misha's clothes, and kept ringing, jumping and running around.

"You have a jolly time," Misha told them, "I'd like to stay with you always. The whole day you don't do a thing. You don't have lessons, or schoolteachers, and you've even got music all day."

"Ding – ding – ding!" shouted the little bells. "And you find it jolly here! No, Misha, we don't have such a nice life. It's true, we don't have any lessons, but what sense is there in that? We wouldn't be afraid of lessons. Our whole trouble is precisely that we – poor old us – we have no real purpose in life. We don't have any books or any pictures; we don't have any mums or dads; nothing to occupy ourselves with; the whole day we just play and play, and do you know, Misha, that can be very, very boring? Take our word for it! Our tortoiseshell sky is very nice, our little gold sun is very nice and so are our gold trees. But, poor old us, we've been looking at all this for so long, and we've got so fed up with it all. From this little town, we can't move an inch, and you can imagine yourself what it's like for a whole age, doing nothing, just sitting in a snuffbox – even in a snuffbox with music."

"Yes," replied Misha, "you are quite right. That even happens to me: when you can get down to your toys after lessons, then it's so enjoyable. But when it's a holiday, and you just play and play, then by the evening it's just boring. You start with one toy and then another – and still it's not much fun. For a long time I never understood why that is, but now I understand."

"Yes, but besides that, we have another rotten thing: we have our wicked uncles."

"What wicked uncles?" asked Misha.

"Our uncles the hammers," replied the little bells, "oh they're so wicked! All the time, they just go around the town and they keep striking us. The bigger ones don't get the 'tap-tap' so often, but the little ones – they don't half have a rough time of it."

And in fact Misha could see some men or other walking along the street on their thin legs, with exceedingly long noses, whispering among themselves: "Tap-tap-tap! Tap-tap-tap! Up you go! Give it to them! Tap-tap-tap!"

And in actual fact these hammering uncles kept on going from one little bell to another with a tapping and a tapping, until Misha began feeling really sorry about the whole thing. He went over to these gentlemen, made a very polite bow, and very good-naturedly asked why they kept striking the poor boys without any mercy at all.

And the hammers said to him in reply:

"Clear off, don't put us off! There in his residence, all in his vestments, our supervisor lurks and he gives us the works. He keeps us bustling, with his constant hassling. Tap-tap-tap! Tap-tap-tap!"

"And what sort of a supervisor is yours?" Misha asked the little bells.

"Oh it's Mister Cylinder," they rang out, "he's a really nice person, he doesn't come down from his sofa, day or night; we can't complain about him."

Misha went over to the supervisor. He looked at him, and he really was lying on his sofa, in his dressing gown, and turning from side to side, though always with his face up. And all over his vestment he had pins, with hooks in great quantity. As soon as he gets hold of a hammer, he first catches it on a hook, then lets it go, and the little hammer will knock against a little bell.

As soon as Misha had gone up to him, the supervisor shouted out:

"Lovey-dovey! Who comes here? Who goes there? Lovey-dovey! Who doesn't go away? Who keeps me awake? Lovey-dovey! Lovey-dovey!"

"It's only me," Misha replied, being really brave, "I – I'm Misha…"

35

"And what are you here for?" asked the supervisor.

"Well, I feel sorry for the poor little bell-boys. They are all so clever, so kind, and such musicians, and because of your commands their uncles keep on striking them..."

"And what's it to me, lovey-dovey! It's not me who's top dog here. Let these uncles knock the boys about! What's it got to do with me? I am a kind supervisor, I just lie on the sofa; I'm really a bit of a loafer. Lovey-dovey, lovey-dovey..."

"Well, I think I have learned a lot in this little town!" Misha said to himself. "But I still get a bit annoyed that for some reason the supervisor doesn't let me out of his sight. 'What a rotten so-and-so,' I think. 'He's not my Mummy or my Daddy. What's it got to do with him, if I'm playing up? If I'd known, I would have stayed in my room.' No, now I can see what happens to poor boys when no one is looking after them."

Meanwhile, Misha had gone on further – and then he stopped. He could see a golden tent with a pearl fringe. On top of it, a golden weathervane was turning, like a wind-mill, and under the tent lay Princess Spring, who, like a snake, coiled up and then uncoiled, and continually prodded the supervisor in the side. Misha was very surprised at this, and he said to her:

"Madam Princess! Why do you prod the supervisor under his side?"

"Sip-sip-sip," replied the princess. "What a stupid boy you are, a foolish boy. You keep on looking at everything, but you see nothing! Were I not to prod the cylinder, the cylinder would not go round. Were the cylinder not to go round, then it wouldn't catch on to the hammers. Were the hammers not to do their striking, the little bells wouldn't do their ringing. Were the bells not to do their ringing, there would be no music! Sip-sip-sip!"

Misha wanted to find out whether the princess was telling the truth. He bent over and pressed her with his finger. And then what happened?

In one instant, the spring untwisted with some force, the cylinder forcibly whirled, the hammers started swiftly striking, the little bells started playing all over the scale, and the spring suddenly snapped. Everything went quiet. The cylinder stopped, the hammers fell back, the little bells curled on to their side, the little sun just hung down, and the little houses were smashed apart... Then Misha remembered that his Papa had told him not to touch the spring, and he got frightened and... he woke up.

"What were you dreaming about, Misha?" asked his Papa.

For a long time Misha didn't know where he was. He looked round: he was in that same room – his Dad's; the snuffbox was still in front of him; beside him his Dad and Mum were sitting, and laughing.

"Where's the little bell-boy? Where's that uncle-hammer? Where's Princess Spring?" asked Misha. "So, was it all a dream?"

"Yes, Misha, the music lulled you off, and you had a really good nap, right here. But, come on now, tell us all about your dream!"

"Well, you see, Dad," said Misha, rubbing his eyes, "I really wanted to find out what makes the music play in the snuffbox. So I set about having a really good look at it, to sort out what moves inside it and what makes it all move. I was thinking and thinking about it, and was just starting to get into things, when suddenly a little door in the snuffbox opened up..." And now Misha told them the whole of his dream, in the order it had all happened.

"Well, now I can see," said his Papa, "that you really do almost understand what makes the music in the snuffbox play. But you will understand it all even better when you come to study mechanics."

THE BLACK GLOVE

1838; dated 1835

Dedicated to Yul. Mikh. Dyugamel

(Kozlovskaya)

I N MY YOUNGER DAYS, I was best man at a certain very interesting wedding. The groom and the bride, seemingly, had been made for one another. Equally young, equally full of life, equally good-looking, both from a good family and – the wonderful thing! – both equally rich. These were two creatures whom fate, it seemed, had released into the world in order not always to be able to be called unmerciful. Fate had showered the young couple from the cradle with all the gifts of happiness, and seemingly had even been fastidious in the choice of these gifts, in each case trying to give them the most perfect form. So, for example, the young couple had a lot of estates and not one lawsuit; they had lots of kind and sincere relations and there was no string of those second-rate relatives, of whose existence a respectable person would only be aware from visiting cards, or through pleading letters or letters of recommendation.

The fathers and mothers of our pair of lovers had long since departed this world. Count Vladimir grew up with his fiancée in the home of their joint guardian and uncle, Akinfy Vasilyevich Ezersky whom, I think, you may have known. If you remember, a rather portly, ruddy-cheeked man, always in a wide, brown tail-coat, slightly powdered, and with the sort of important and decisive face that somewhat resembles Franklin. It was in his place that my young people lived. Almost from their cradles they never parted, one from the other, and from early on, in their guardian's mind, they were set to be husband and wife.

Akinfy Vasilyevich Ezersky was a highly remarkable man in many respects: nature had given him intellect and a kind heart. Unfortunately, nature gives us just eyes, but makes us invent lenses ourselves, which are able to see slightly further than our natural vision. Such lenses Akinfy Vasilyevich did not receive in childhood. He was taught in the old-fashioned way: he was made to learn by heart geographical names, historical dates, moralistic maxims and fortification measurements – but they forgot to teach him one thing: to think about what he was being taught. Such instruction, as is always the case, told upon him for his whole life: what his natural mind saw and his heart felt – that was what his education could not see through to the end. Thus he thought only with half of his head, felt with half of his heart, and thus he frequently understood only half of a subject.

After such a strange upbringing, fate threw him over to England, where he spent several years of his life. This new world could not but affect him, but, as with a savage, he was affected equally by the good and the bad; the one and the other for him became confused. There was much that he overlooked in the one and in the other, much that he looked over again, and both the one and the other he brought back whole to Russian soil. So, for example, notwithstanding the gibes of ignoramuses, or the mockery of writers who were not ashamed to support with their pen the opinion of illiterates, and to display in their works the triumph of ingrained stupidity over essential improvement, Ezersky brought into the estates of his nurslings a refined management and, as if to spite illiterate neighbours, illiterate tales and comedies, increased his receipts tenfold. But together with that he brought back to his household the shoots of a dry sort of methodism which more or less

39

tells upon the whole of English life and kills off in it any kind of poetry.

Hastily, he read through Bentham* and the idea of *benefit* became a dazzling sun for Ezersky; it made dark stains on his own thoughts. Man seemed to him a machine that was then only happy when operating during fixed hours and for a known purpose. Poetry to him seemed trash, the imagination a demon which needed to be avoided. Any uncalculated impulse of the heart was all but sinful. But fortunately, he also managed to read Thomson,* and the idea of the beauty of nature mixed in his head with Benthamite industrialism. In this manner, Akinfy Vasilyevich constructed for himself a system that was a mixture of Bentham, Thomson, Paley* and other English authors whom he used to read in his youth; the newer ones he did not know and therefore did not like. Byron* he hated, because Byron cursed England – which for Akinfy Vasilyevich, together with his own system, was the model of perfection. Uncle often explained his system, but to grasp it was rather difficult. To the idea that benefit had to be the basis of any human action he added an inexpressible attachment to nature and voiced his rapture with verses from *The Seasons*. Everything in nature seemed to him perfection and he often went on about the necessity for living, as he said, "in conformity with nature". As a consequence of this, he got carried away by every hillock, every warped tree. But this "methodism" did not make him forget himself in this delight: he constantly went to bed at ten o'clock, got up with the sun and read Thomson's verses to it. After the verses, he drank tea, smoked two cigars (never more, never less) and sat down to work, which would go on until three. At three o'clock he would go out for a walk and for dinner; even when he dined alone, he would go out in a white cravat and shoes.

There was clearly expressed in all his activities this English one-sidedness that – thank God – is incomprehensible to a Russian person. From this come all the merits and all the shortcomings of these English works, from which an Englishman knows the pair of wheels in a machine, and a pair of thoughts in life; he knows these only too well, but, beyond this, he is able to make no sense at all of anything else in the world. Despite these peculiarities, the habit for work and order gave Akinfy Vasilyevich an important advantage over all his peers. Only he was capable of doing what ten others could not do. Just because of this, he had masses to do. He enjoyed bustling about, just as others enjoyed doing nothing. And as there were thousands of enthusiasts of the latter type, Ezersky was a big social trustee, the president of all possible commissions to do with the affairs of his acquaintances, and the intermediary in all disputes.

Of course, the upbringing which he provided for his charges conformed to his system. He schooled Maria in the cultivation of feminine wares and feminine humility, and the young Count in all mercantile and gymnastic exercises. Thus Maria became a wonderful maker of tea and the most refined bread and butter slices; she was fully versed in plum pudding and mince pies; and the Count knew trigonometry and book-keeping, boxed splendidly, rode a horse and could climb up ropes. Moreover, both of them knew several grammars almost by heart. Their upbringing was, as you can see, of a most practical nature, most down to earth, based not on ideas, but on benefit. Indeed, no other type of book, no other thought, came into their hands or into their heads; only a month before their wedding did Akinfy Vasilyevich allow the spouses-to-be to read Richardson's *Clarissa*.*

The wedding of Count Vladimir and Maria was not exactly a novelty for the town, but everyone genuinely welcomed it. In both of them, there was something inexplicably innocent, inexplicably infantile. These were two little childish heads, drawn by a skilful London engraver, which you can't help but love, forgetting that into these splendid creations had already been planted the seed of that moral arithmetic over which Byron had shed such bitter tears. Indeed, there was in them a kind of magnetism, which produced the effect that no one resented them, no one grumbled to Fate upon seeing their happiness, but looked upon it as a young people's right to possession. It is true that crowds of young people whirled around the beautiful Maria, that women involuntarily stared at the stately Vladimir; but this was surprise, not jealousy, and not annoyance. With their childlike appearance, they were able to excite only the pure, clear surface of the soul, leaving at the bottom its black, heavy drops. Their wedding seemed to be a joyful children's holiday, of the sort that everyone admires and no one resents.

The ceremony finished. Vladimir tenderly kissed his Maria. Almost the whole city has assembled in the church and the house. They congratulated the newlyweds but by twelve o'clock all had departed, leaving the young couple in freedom. Their uncle, who had taken the place of a father for them, and other fathers and mothers likewise seated around, having performed their domestic rites, had drifted away. The young couple were already in the bedroom and with childlike innocence were feasting their eyes on the furnishing of the room, which until then had been kept secret from them, when suddenly on the white satin divan they spotted a black glove. At first Vladimir thought that one of the guests had forgotten it, but who could ever think of coming to a wedding with a black glove? With a certain sense of supernatural fear, he lifted it and could feel within it a letter, which bore an inscription in the name of them both. In some alarm, Vladimir ripped off the seal and read the following:

I consider it necessary to inform you that your happiness disturbs my happiness, that the fulfilment of your desires destroys all the plans of my life. And since it is pardonable for a person to love himself more than others, then I have proposed to myself the firm principle of turning your wedding inside out, for only by your suffering can I achieve my aim. Should I not be successful in this, then at least I shall have the enjoyment of taking revenge on you, and this first visit is only the first step in that evil which I am preparing for you. Only your separation at the very minute that you begin reading this note can save you from my vengeance. This token left by me may show you that neither doors nor bolts exist for me. Take the liberty of picking it up, oh over-happy couple!

The Black Glove

At first Vladimir did not want to show this letter to Maria, but Maria, leaning on his shoulder, had been able to read the whole of it to the end.

"It's probably a joke... a hoax," said Vladimir in a faint voice; but his hand was unintentionally shaking.

"No," answered Maria, "it's not a joke and not a hoax; who would joke with us so cruelly?"

"But who would wish us harm?" remarked Vladimir.

"Think, have you insulted anyone? Is there anyone to whom you haven't kept any promises?"

Here Maria looked meaningfully at Vladimir, and her voice broke.

"And you can really think that, Maria?" Vladimir said tenderly. "I assure you that it's a joke, a stupid joke, which will not go without answer. If it's a woman, then never mind; but if it's a man, then..." And Vladimir's eyes sparkled.

"And then, what?" asked Maria.

"Oh, nothing!" said Vladimir, "I'll just try to pay him back in the same coin."

"No, that's not what your eyes are saying... Listen, Vladimir, promise me not to do anything without telling me first."

"Oh, what do we need these promises for?"

"Promise me, at least, not to undertake anything before tomorrow."

"Oh, we really are children!" said Vladimir, laughing. "Some stupid mischief-maker has played a joke on us and we, as though in subservience to him, have spent a whole hour in alarm."

"And if he's here and listening to us?" asked Maria.

"That really hadn't entered my head," said Vladimir. With these words, he took up a candle, walked round the room and opened the door, so as to go out of the bedroom.

"Don't go alone," said Maria, " – we should call the servants."

"Do you want them to start laughing at us?"

"Well, then, let's go together."

They left the bedroom. The fires were out everywhere. Everyone in the house was asleep; in the courtyard could be heard only the watchman's wooden staff. Around the large rooms trailed a long shadow from the candle. Maria unwittingly shuddered when her own image chanced to get reflected in the mirrors, when an echo repeated the rustle of their steps, and a glimmering light momentarily produced on the folds of brocade whimsical outlines. Thus did they go round the whole house. Everything was quiet, so they returned to the bedroom; by then three o'clock had already sounded and, when Vladimir drew back the curtain, dawn was already breaking.

The light of day has a wonderful quality: it delivers to us an involuntary cheerfulness and brings tranquillity to our common sense. That which seems enormous and horrible in the darkness of night will dribble away in the light of day, like a dream. This was the feeling experienced by our young people.

"We really are children," Vladimir repeated once again. "Who would ever have seen a first wedding night spent over a silly letter?"

Upon these words, he went over to the fireplace and almost threw the glove into it, but held himself back on the thought that it wouldn't be a bad idea to show it to their uncle.

"Can this nonsense really shake the foundations of our happiness?"

"Never!" replied Maria, clasping him in her arms.

The next day the young couple did not forget to show the mysterious note to their uncle. Uncle took a look at it with his usual systematic composure and said: "This is some kind of nonsense, but something which, however, should not just be left like that. Give this note to me. There is nothing for you to be doing about it; this is now going to be my business."

We have already mentioned that Uncle was a highly remarkable man in his own way and that his strict order in life, his unalterable composure in the most difficult circumstances, and his several successful financial turnovers gained him the trust of all his acquaintances. Indeed, when he came out with: "This is now going to be my business," in his firm methodical voice, with a stress on every word, then it was impossible not to believe him.

When all the newlyweds' visits had been accomplished, Akinfy Vasilyevich insisted that the young couple should, without fail, set off for the country. He had really wanted to send them there on the first day after their marriage, in the English way, but, for the first time in his life, against his will, he gave way to the insistent requests from relatives.

"Drive off into the country," Akinfy Vasilyevich told them. "In the first place, you must get to know one another, and, in the second place, no person in this world should live uselessly. You, Vladimir, must get on to management. Remember that every proprietor of land in this world must constantly increase its productive strength, and that he who does not annually increase his income loses all that he could have gained. I am deliberately not going with you: I want you to be able to get used to your own strengths, not relying on anyone's help, so that when I die – for death is the inevitable and beneficial law of nature – you will not notice your loss."

"Uncle, can you really talk about that so composedly?"

"It's nothing, nothing, just empty words. Death is the law of nature, and everything in nature is splendid; people have to die," Uncle added in a significant manner, "so people have to be born; and so," he went on, "you will devote yourself to estate management, and you too, Maria. In the country home, in the study, on the writing desk, you will find a notebook, which I filled out for you ten years ago now, in which it is noted down in detail what a husband has to do, and what a wife has to do. Follow all my advice exactly, and you won't regret it. At first it will seem hard, but then everything will get easier and easier. In the most difficult instances, get back to me with your questions. More than anything, try to restrain your passions, and even to eliminate them altogether – after that everything will be easy. I shall be in the Siberian village, as spending the summer in town is a crime. Here you can't see nature, and what can compare with nature? 'Nothing rouses the soul like the rising of the sun,' says Thomson. Now, off you go, with God's grace! Your travelling carriage is ready – I organized its construction myself – and the horses have already been brought round."

Vladimir and Maria threw themselves tearfully into Uncle's arms, but he cut them short: "We need neither tears nor farewells. All that is just useless branches which the intelligent gardener has to cut off thoroughly..."

However, Vladimir and Maria did not listen to the strict counselling of Uncle, and cried their fill. Eventually they took their seats in the carriage and Uncle went off to his rooms, since he had not yet had time to smoke his second cigar.

We shall not follow our travellers along their lengthy road, along the slopes, under the broken bridges. We shall not stop for bits of damage to the coach, for arguments with postmasters and the endless sorting out of coachmen. We shall presuppose that they got to their country village in that blessed time when Russia will be crossed in all directions by railways – which was impatiently awaited not only by Akinfy Vasilyevich, notwithstanding the wise commentaries of various thinkers who imagine that, with the coming of the railways, the so humble and industrious class of coach-drivers will be exterminated. In their village, under the blessed sky of Tambov province, across which, not in a joke but in actual fact, moves a clear warm sun, the young couple found their house, constructed with all the enlightened conveniences of life. In the study, on the writing desk, really was to be found the notebook placed there ten years before, written in Akinfy Vasilyevich's hand. We cannot forgo the pleasure of copying out a few pages from this truly practical notebook:

> *Husband and wife are two halves of one and the same being; but each has their own special qualities and duties and in their own way must further the attainment of the single goal of nature and society – common benefit.*
>
> *Husband and wife get up at the one time. In the summer they immediately go into the fresh air and enjoy nature. Nothing so reinforces a person's strengths, required for daily tasks, as a splendid situation, lit up by the beams of a rising sun, when the whole of nature is coming to life and every little flower sings a hymn to the Almighty...*

After this there followed a few verses from Thomson, and at the end the note:

> *In the winter, the couple remain in their room.*
>
> *At seven o'clock the spouses take breakfast (tea or coffee). After breakfast, the husband goes off to look through the day's work. Among his occupations belong the arable land, the garden, the meadows, the kitchen-gardens – on which more detail is given in the notebook under No. 26. The wife's management is concerned with all the domestic business: the*

milk yard, the kitchen, the laundry house, various types of domestic hand-making – on which more detail is given in the notebook under No. 28.

By midday all instructions must be completed, and the spouses join one another in the dining room for a second breakfast (bread, butter and cold roast beef). And, as it may be noticed that all animals give themselves over to sleep before midday, from this it must be concluded that that is what is demanded by beneficial nature – therefore spouses too must dedicate this time to rest...

We shall not prolong this extract, but we may rest assured that our young couple read the whole notebook with due respect, and did not laugh at it even once.

However, the fulfilment of Uncle's instructions did not have the same success. This started with the young couple sleeping in on the first day, from the road, until midday. From this, the whole day fell into disorder. They did not manage to delight in nature on time; they went out for a walk at the time of common natural sleep; they breakfasted at half-past one, as a result of which they were compelled to dine at eight; after this they wandered around right up to midnight and went to bed after two o'clock in the morning. From all this, the next day they again slept in until midday and in such manner, imperceptibly, every day went past in twisted fashion. The fixing of work tasks fell in the time when the workers had their rest period; the visitation to the cattle yard when all the cows were at pasture, and so on. Messages from the stewards were put aside; eventually they piled up so much that it became impossible to get them read. Little by little, the English systematic management turned into the common way of life of the Russian landlord, whereby everything gets ruined, gets eaten up and drunk up, and no one knows about anything or cares, relying on Orthodox-style *living*, which *lives through* a lot more than any possible luxury.

It is no wonder that estate management soon got the young Count down. Furthermore, he and the Countess unexpectedly noticed that they had become bored, that it was coming to pass for them to spend the entire day eye to eye, saying nothing. This happened perfectly naturally and from a very simple cause: because they had nothing to talk about. People with developed imagination and feelings live through an entire age and will always find something new to say to each other; but it is not possible to talk all day about horses or buttered tartlets. And since the spouses had nothing to talk about, they began to grumble at each other; but since it's not possible to grumble for an entire age, they would start to quarrel out of boredom, but eventually even this amusing occupation would start getting on their nerves. Fortunately, the Count found himself something to do: in the district there were many hunters with hounds. He got to know them, badgered foxes and hares, and drank for two – in the Russian and the English styles. The young Countess got acquainted with her female neighbours who, however, bored her to death, and with whom she soon fell out. The Countess began unintentionally recalling Moscow drawing rooms and the Moscow theatre. In these pursuits there passed the summer and part of the autumn.

Meanwhile, there occurred a minor incident, which produced a complete turn around in the Count's thinking. In that province, elections were under way. A number of the Count's admirers, of whom for any rich man there are always plenty, came to him with plans and arguments, as to how gratifying it would be for them, and for their concerns, and how honourable for the Count, were he to agree to be leader of their administrative council unit. This idea very much appealed to the young Count; there was something new in it, and everything old had already greatly bored him. He gave his consent with great condescension. In his head already swirled plans for the transformation of the whole district, for there was something

Uncle-like in the young Count, diluted by our commonplace frivolity and laziness. Soon this idea completely overcame the rest of his imagination, and the title of "Leader" even came into his dreams at night. On the day appointed for the election, the Count donned his uniform and presented himself, firmly confident of being elected. But what a blow it was to him when another was chosen instead of him! He could not regain his senses from amazement..

"What does this mean?" he asked one person and another: "What advantage does my rival have? He is not richer, or perhaps cleverer, is he?…"

One refused to answer, another just beat about the bush, many others laughed quietly, with all their provincial malice, at the residents from the capital.

"I'll tell you," finally said one rather older neighbour. "What's to blame here is not the nobility, but you. Your rival is a serving official of rank, while you, your honour, you know, excuse me, do not hold any post or rank."

"No rank!" exclaimed the Count. "No post?" – and he hurriedly departed from the meeting. These few words opened up for him a whole world, the existence of which he had not even suspected.

In actual fact, Uncle, in accordance with his English system, had not at all presupposed that his nephew would ever really need to enter government service properly. He wanted to make out of him an excellent agronomist, what he called "a proprietor of the land", and he imagined that it would be quite sufficient for the Count to be in the service for a year or two, as a formality, and then to live on his estate like an English lord or farmer.

Well, indeed – life is splendid, but not for us. Vladimir was so accustomed to Uncle's care regarding everything, in all that concerned him, so used to thinking in terms of his ideals, that when Uncle had told him: "it's not possible both to be in the service and to take care of one's land-owning affairs", or "an owner of land is obliged to dedicate his entire life to the improvement of his property" – it never entered Vladimir's head to raise any objection with Akinfy Vasilyevich. Simply, on the very next day, he had put in his resignation and left the service with the title of Civil Service Clerk, 14th Class.

The incident of the elections strongly affected the young man. His self-regard, which had already begun to stir with the expectation of the leadership position, was now even more strongly disturbed. Our general disease, love of rank or, if you prefer, love of ambition, began little by little to creep into his soul. It already seemed to him that passers-by on the road did not bow to him properly: because he saw with what deference at the elections they all wrapped themselves round the new leader, because he noticed what effect was produced on those around by crosses and stars – not so noticeable in the capitals. In these few hours, Vladimir aged ten years. "What am I doing, rotting in this village!" he said to himself: "I need to be in the service, I need to gain ranks, crosses, stars, splendours, honours."

Gradually there began in his mind those calculations that serve as a normal, constant preoccupation for inveterate civil servants. He counted up the number of years he had lost to no purpose, became annoyed with Uncle and at his English system, at himself, at his marriage – to put it in a nutshell, at everything in the social world.

He returned home extremely out of sorts. Maria was also fed up with her neighbours and their tales of various provincial scandals, which usually pertain at the time of elections – so Maria was also not in good spirits. That evening they again quarrelled – what for, they didn't know themselves. It was simply because they had to quarrel, each to vent their spleen on someone's heart – this being one of the advantages of the matrimonial condition.

The point is that, on the next day, both started talking, little by little, about the necessity of leaving the village. But how were they to announce this desire to Uncle, who wrote to them by every post, reminding them what estate work had to be got on with at that time, going on about the importance of farming in general and the beauty of countryside nature in particular?

One eventuality brought them out of their difficulty: Maria became pregnant. The couple did not delay in informing Uncle of this and declaring to him that the Countess's condition demanded absolutely that they should move back to Moscow or Petersburg.

Although Uncle very much felt like leaving the Countess's pregnancy to the salutary force of nature, having thought it over a bit, he accepted that it would be for the best to agree to the young people's request and, in place of nature, to rely on a good obstetrician. Moreover, his guardianship business was calling himself personally to Petersburg, and so finally he nominated this city as the place for meeting up with the young ones.

The young people were waiting only for this, and decided to travel away that very day, despite the bad roads. He was gratified by daydreams of ranks and crosses, she by Petersburg balls. But in the midst of these merry preparations they received a letter, sealed with a black stamp. Vladimir wanted to hide this letter, but Maria had caught sight of it, and – is it possible not to satisfy a woman's curiosity? This letter contained the following few words:

You are now at the height of your bliss; you will soon be a father and mother; you will succeed in everything, all will be fulfilled in accordance with your desires. But, be careful and remember that your enemy does not slumber, and that your every happiness is for him a new cause to hate you and to prepare for you in secret all kinds of harm.

The Black Glove

This letter staggered the young people. They could not comprehend who could be to them such an inveterate enemy. In the words "succeed in everything", Vladimir saw his failure at the elections: he suspected the hand of this infuriated Glove in that event. All the more did he want, as they say, to get on in the world and with his own weight crush this importunate enemy. Another feeling was torturing Maria: the curiosity to find out who this Black Glove was and what could be the reason for its strange persecution. She hoped that this riddle could sooner be resolved in the capital than in this backward place. You can see that Maria has also become much more experienced.

Be that as it may, all these thoughts did not prevent the preparations for their departure. They respectfully replaced Uncle's notebook in its previous place and took their seats in the carriage. With regret they looked out at their surrounding menials, who were shedding buckets of tears, though secretly, of course being pleased that their masters were going away – several of the faithful servants were already half-drunk out of joy, and they cried the loudest of all.

After a lengthy journey, our spouses drove into Petersburg, which presented itself to them in all its splendour: rain, slush, hoarfrost – it was the first of May.

They found Uncle already in Petersburg. This man, born for ceaseless activity, had already managed to prepare everything for them. A house in the best part of town, which even sometimes got the sun, furniture, full domestic staff, and even a midwife and an obstetrician – his indefatigable thoughtfulness had foreseen everything. The first days our young couple spent rather tediously. They had to give Uncle an account of everything they had done, tell all about what they hadn't got round to, and cover up the real reason for their journey to Petersburg. From all this, was born in their little circle a sort of restraint. Had they been in another town, Uncle would soon have guessed that his young couple aspired not to become English farmers, but that they simply wanted, as is said in Russia, to live a bit.

But Petersburg life, where everything is given over to just a minute in the day, and then flawed, where a person resembles a threshing machine that knocks and crackles ceaselessly, until it breaks completely – amid such a way of life, it was easy for the young couple to steer clear of Uncle's acumen.

Soon our young couple aged a bit within this life. The Countess threw herself into this abyss with a craving for delights, noise, diversity, dances, flirtations; as did the Count, with a released fresh passion for ambition. He soon comprehended all the secrets of this variegated world; he soon taught himself the art of drawing attention to himself, of biding his time, of knowing whose acquaintance to make, and upon whom to turn his back. He learned those phrases that are at times worth throwing in the air, learned the right moment to buy and the right moment to sell, learned to lie a little bit, to tell tales a little bit, and to slander a little bit. He did not rush, did not complain, but, like a skilful commander, held his trenches.

The Countess's delivery time put a stop for a while to these pursuits of the married couple. Uncle, until this time calm, sure of the complete success of his superior system, finally began to suspect that something was being kept from him. For example, he was very surprised when the young Count was not able to enlighten him on the balance of debt and credit of the Tambov village, nor to explain to him what effect had been produced during the harvesting by the forest sown by Akinfy Vasilyevich about ten years ago. But how surprised was he when on one occasion his nephew showed him the letter from a certain significant man, in which the Count was invited to enter the service, and when straight after this the Count with ardour began trying to prove to him his innate bent for the diplomatic service, and when he started counting out to him on his fingers all the advantages awaiting him! All this was coming at the very same minute when Vladimir was getting ready to be a father, "the head of a domestic state, the natural mentor and supervisor of his children", as Akinfy Vasilyevich said when the obstetrician was already right by the Countess's room. Akinfy Vasilyevich was amazed, startled and, for the first time in his life, his voice lost its usual firmness and determination. He was even at a loss as to what to reply to the young man of ambition. The first step had been taken.

The birth reached its conclusion successfully in itself, only the child died shortly afterwards. The midwife said this was because the Countess had over-tightly laced herself and danced too much just before her labour, but the obstetrician said that the baby died through not having the resources for the continuation of its life.

The Countess quickly recovered. It was the time of Lenten abstinence. Balls had stopped and the Countess attended morning concert rehearsals, since she could not as yet don her evening dresses. One day the Countess was feeling bored in the morning; the wind was blowing in the courtyard, and a blizzard was blowing similarly on the street, as it does in the life and the head of Petersburgers. The Countess was expecting no callers. She took a look at her huge sheet of notices; some bright spark was seemingly playing some folk instrument at a concert, but this was all the same to the Countess: she just wanted something to drive out to. The Count was long since not in the house.

There was not much going on in the concert hall. The Countess was over-dressed, as usual. The recognition that she was a mother who had lost her baby, that she was young, attractive-looking, and that she had recently recovered from bad health, imparted to the Countess both a moral and a physical languor. She flaunted her indisposition and her misfortune. While the Countess was strolling around the hall, a passing face was glimpsed that seemed vaguely familiar. Beside this figure was another, one that indeed was familiar to her. This latter person was one of those people who, it seems, chase after one everywhere, one whom you meet all over the place. You run into them on your morning visits, and at dinners, before the *soirée* and at the *soirée*, and even at night, in the carriage standing by the entrance. These are people who ask about everything and everyone, answer about everything and everyone, and who are ready to speak even with our commentators on morals, unafraid of their serious and subtle powers of observation. This gentleman, naturally, was one of the Countess's callers. His eagle-like gaze immediately took note of a lady acquaintance. He lost no time in going up to her with his usual array of questions.

"With whom were you talking just now?" the Countess asked him.

"It was your long-standing friend, Vorotynsky."

"Long-standing friend," repeated the Countess: "about ten years back I used to dance with him at the children's balls, and since those days I have completely lost sight of him."

"He, this very minute, was asking me to introduce him to you... May I?"

"Oh, without a doubt."

A young man came over, trying to remember what he had long since forgotten, various adventures of childhood, and he remarked jokingly that even then he was already running after the Countess and asked for permission to carry on doing so. The Countess laughed, trying also to show that she remembered all that had long been forgotten, when suddenly, amid a most torrid conversation, she stopped short in involuntary embarrassment. She had noticed that there were black gloves on Vorotynsky. The young man noticed the strange reaction produced by him on Maria and also became involuntarily confused; but the Countess, a society lady, immediately came to her senses and coolly asked:

"What do these black gloves mean? Are you really in mourning?"

"In mourning, Countess."

"For whom?"

"Oh, permit me not to reply to that question: you would just laugh."

"Do you really think that I am of such a merry disposition?"

"That's how it seems to me: you are so happy."

At this phrase the Countess was again made to think, but immediately she responded with a new question:

"Tell me, for whom are you in mourning?"

"If you really want to know that, then I'll tell you, Countess, but on condition that you do not laugh."

"Oh, come, come! I really must know: for whom are you in mourning?"

"For myself," the young man said with a weighty air.

The Countess started to guffaw. "Have you really died, then?"

"I told you that you would laugh."

"Your words are either nothing but a joke, or they are very important."

"Neither the one thing, nor the other, Countess; in life everything intermingles."

"You talk about life as though you know it."

"I do know it, and have done so for a very long time."

"You are not married?"

"No."

"In that case, you don't know anything."

These last words had unintentionally escaped from the Countess's lips. They both fell silent. I don't know what was going on in the soul of the young man; and it would be difficult to find out. He belonged to the category of those people of the new generation who are able to laugh without smiling and cry without tears; those who, seemingly, cannot be surprised or moved by anything – and this is not from dissembling, but out of habit. Not one feeling would come out from him on to the surface, not a single movement would betray the incomprehensible secret of his soul. He could speak of the most bitter feeling with an indifferent smile, of the most joyful with a scorn which, apparently, replied in advance to any questions from the inquisitive. His appeal was, like his clothing, simple – without any pretensions and methodically buttoned up. He was pale, his dark curly hair set off the cold, almost lifeless, features of his face. Only occasionally did some sort of a momentary light sparkle in his eyes and then die out in the same instant. Whether there was grief in his heart, or simply the aristocratic world's custom of feeling nothing or, in the end, a mere fashionableness, it would be difficult to divine. All of this is so mixed up in the new generation which, seemingly, has set itself the rule of being a riddle to everyone and, perhaps, most of all to itself.

He produced an astonishing impression on the Countess. Vaguely, it appeared to her that between this new acquaintance and the Black Glove there existed some kind of a link. Her feminine self-regard was flattered by the thought that she had engendered towards herself an exclusive hatred, which a secret, barely audible voice was expressing to her in a different manner. She was terrified, and tormented with fascination. It was the latter feeling that won out.

The music again tied the thread of the severed conversation. The wretched artiste, toiling away with the orchestra, could never have expected that, with a false note, he would have provided grounds for an explanation between two people who had been so divided by space and time. This false note was reminiscent of the violinist, playing during the dancing lessons at which the Countess and Vorotynsky used to meet. This violinist brought back the circumstances, which the Countess had totally forgotten, in which Vorotynsky, in his childhood, always used to wear a bandage round his face. This bandage brought back the way that all the children used to shun the poor unfortunate one, and gave Vorotynsky grounds for telling the Countess how fate had pursued him from his very childhood. At this point, the conversation started to clutch at every word.

The Countess until now had seen around her rich, healthy, rosy-cheeked people, pleased with themselves, for whom misfortune consisted in losing a game at whist. In the middle of this contentment, the Countess had at times felt bored, but from what exactly, she didn't understand. She did not dare call herself unhappy: to come out with this word would have seemed to her strange and indecent. Vorotynsky, talking about himself, had explained her own feeling to her, and gave life and word to the vague sensations of her soul. He told her about *the unhappiness of being happy*, of the misfortune of being rich, the misfortune of being in need of nothing, the misfortune of fulfilling all one's desires, the misfortune of living for a few years in foreign lands, and finally of those secret, inexplicable misfortunes which gravitate towards the soul of a person of intelligence and sensibility. For example, the misfortune of listening to good music, the misfortune of looking at a good painting, the misfortune of reading good verses and generally the misfortune of living – in short, all these misfortunes which are very funny in novels and tales, but which are in reality also essential, in which in the same way you involuntarily believe, just like those circumstances which in society enjoy the label of being "unfortunate".

The Countess understood all this, although these words were new for her. She listened attentively to them, like a future renegade does to the words of a man converting him to his own schism. She often wanted to direct the conversation on to the subject that so fascinated her; but the young man knew how to evade questions: they served him only as a step towards what he wanted to tell the Countess. He skilfully left an idea unexplained, a word in reticence – and by this means told her quite a lot more than he was saying.

"Stupid readers!" once shouted the Abbot Galiani,* "you read only what is written in black upon white, only the lines; learn to read white upon black, and you'll be able to read between the lines."

Vorotynsky possessed this skill to perfection: in the gaps between his words were other words, which he didn't pronounce, but which a mysterious voice whispered into the ear of the Countess.

However that may have been, the Countess returned home with the thought that she was rich, young and attractive, that her husband was a healthy, rosy-cheeked man, who rode a horse well and boxed splendidly, and that therefore she was very, very unhappy. She delighted in repeating to herself this new, and to her fresh, word. She tried to recall all the events of her life and to seek out their dark side. She found that, in all the enjoyments that she had experienced up to now, something for her was lacking – in a word, she returned home convinced that she was very, very unhappy. The Count was not at home; he had sent word to say that he should not be expected for dinner. This pleased the Countess very much. In confirmation of her unhappiness, she did not order dinner to be served for her, but threw herself into an armchair in her parlour and set about admiring her unhappiness, like a child with a new toy. She picked up first one book and then another, but reading was not for her; her novel was in her head – other people's novels seemed to her dry and cold. At eleven o'clock the Count returned with a flushed face and in very jolly humour. He had been at an improvised luncheon with chance acquaintances and things were going very well for him. The Count went into his wife's parlour with a loud laugh and a dozen puns that he had picked up during the luncheon. This entrance disturbed and distressed the Countess. He had ruined her bitter tranquillity and, when the Count threw himself on to the bed and fell asleep, the Countess remained in her armchair, inclined her head on to the cold marble table, and said quietly: "How unhappy I am, how unhappy I am!"

The morning daybreak caught the Countess in this posture. By now an involuntarily unclear thought was running through her head. She swiftly ran up to the mirror and with horror noticed that the pallor and exhaustion of her face had passed that stage at which indisposition ceases, in a woman, to be interesting. She hurriedly twirled her long chestnut-coloured hair and, from fear, even felt a bit hungry. With slow steps she went through to the dining room, then to the refreshment room, and was very pleased when she found there a forgotten cold dish and – oh dear! – with considerable appetite she ate, and then lay down on her bed and went fast asleep.

I know that some of my readers will consider such behaviour on the part of my Countess completely improper: the heroine is hungry! The heroine eats away! It can't be helped! "Such is the law of beneficial nature!" as Akinfy Vasilyevich would say. I also fear that my readers might think that I am laughing at the poor Countess, or that I am deliberately presenting her in a ridiculous manner: that idea is far from my imagination. No, I understand the Countess's sufferings, I believe in them; these sufferings, I repeat, are essential, for any suffering can be measured only by the organism of that being that it is affecting. There is no doubt that an insect, whose whole nervous system consists of a single thread, suffers little; what a difference with a human being, whose whole body is entangled with nerves! It is the same thing in the moral world: in some the soul is made from tortoiseshell; flick it as much as you like – what does it matter! In another, the soul is more tender than an optic membrane; touch it with a feather, and it will fly into a tremble… Just imagine a young girl with a fiery imagination, with deep sensitivity, brought up by a man like Akinfy Vasilyevich, to whom education meant to rear, to make rich, and who, as we have already said, understood all the physical demands of life, but not a single one of the heart. He would react to the soul like a person who, wishing to preserve his arm from danger of dislocation, would bind it up for several years without moving it.

With the Count, this operation succeeded completely, as he had been born clumsy, but with the Countess it was another matter. For a long time she participated in almost nothing, whatever was done with her; but then her minute came, and what had been missing in her upbringing by Uncle got supplemented of its own accord. Whose fault was it, if this new upbringing was the opposite way round from normal? The Countess's first teacher was boredom; then came a secret sense of discontent, dark and inexpressible; then fascination, aroused by a man in black gloves; and then the enjoyment of listening to him or, to put it better, of talking with his words – words which she previously had not heard and which were as sweet to her as the sounds of one's homeland in a foreign country... Don't accuse the poor Countess, don't laugh at her. Much in her suffering may have seemed ridiculous to those passing by, but she suffered, just as suffers a poor tender animal from a southern homeland, brought by an indifferent trainer to the cold north in a numbered box. A sarcastic Nature mixes up any kind of suffering with something ridiculous: there is a smile on the face of a corpse.

Here we are at two o'clock in the afternoon. Gleaming carriages are racing along the noisy street. The sun is shining into the damask curtains in the splendid dining room; the furniture is arranged in disorder, but with a certain refinement. Why does this young woman, dressed in a rich peignoir trimmed with lace, incessantly keep getting up from her place? Why does she go first up to the window, and then in front of the mirror adjust her hair, which is done up in a four-cornered fashion? She is in some agitation; she is waiting for something unusual and then trying to assure herself that she is calm, and that this day is just like yesterday... But then the bell rang. "Vorotynsky," announced the waiter on entering. The Countess threw herself into an armchair; her heart was beating strongly, but her face was placid and cold. This visit was a short one. By now these were not people who had met by chance and, like members of a Masonic lodge, recognized each other by secret signs. No, these were thrifty traders who wish to hide, one from the other – one the secret of buying, the other the secret of selling. They talked about the most unremarkable subjects; the conversation broke off at every minute, but captivated them both. After half an hour, Vorotynsky got up; the Countess said to him just one thing: "*Au revoir, j'espère*" – but at these words blood rushed to the young man's head.

The Countess holds evenings and musical mornings; the Countess is very fond of picnics and cavalcades; young men and young ladies participate in all these amusements. The Count almost always accompanies his wife, but somehow always remains at the back, beside a certain young lady, while the horses make off in front with the Countess and Vorotynsky. Or, the opposite can happen: the Count will gallop off ahead and the Countess will stay at the back; on these occasions, minor misfortunes generally occur; the Countess's horse will get unbridled or the stirrup will come loose. Such things could have unpleasant consequences, but fortunately at such a time beside the Countess is Vorotynsky, who puts all this into order. He calls himself the Countess's groom – *l'écuyer de Madame*. And others as well call him this.

Time moves on, and very merrily. Summer passed; it is well known that all the seeds of intrigue are sown on the Petersburg soil in summer at the dachas under the noise of the pouring rain, flower in the autumn and ripen in winter. The skilful gardener knows how to cultivate this plant in a single summer; but the Count, like a still inexperienced person, was in need of more time. Be that as it may, one morning he rode over to his Uncle with the announcement that he had got a position in the ***. Uncle sighed, and could only murmur:

"And the estate?"

"But what about you, Uncle?" replied the young man.

"I am now getting old," replied Uncle, " – all that I can do is to try and sell it."

"That wouldn't be a bad idea," replied the Count, "but there is one small hindrance: it's mortgaged."

"Mortgaged!" exclaimed Uncle. "Did you really have in view some sort of beneficial speculation?"

"Yes, my dear Uncle, and something which was completely successful."

"How pleased I am, my dearest friend," said Uncle, "that you have turned to the true path, and what a slyboots! You kept your reckonings from me. Now, tell me quickly what your speculation consists of."

"I've already told you what it is, Uncle..."

"What? When?" the old fellow exclaimed.

"Well, my appointment to a position?"

Akinfy Vasilyevich shook his head.

"It's not possible for me to take care of your estate," he said sadly, "and without proprietorial eyes everything will go topsy-turvy. But still, if your estate is mortgaged only to the public purse, then it can be sold, and with benefit."

"Ah, yes!" said the Count, "but it is mortgaged both to the public purse and to private hands."

"Your speculation has cost you dear!"

"It wasn't cheap, Uncle; you don't get something good for nothing."

At another time, Akinfy Vasilyevich would have got angry, but now he was in the position of a man unexpectedly flying down a staircase to the last step. He was struck dumb, all his thoughts dried up; out came only his natural purity of heart, and he exclaimed:

"Very well, it's impossible to live without money: I won't abandon you."

Meanwhile, in the Countess's house another scene was going on. The Countess, in a reverie, tears in her eyes, sits in an armchair, while Vorotynsky walks around the room with big steps.

"Countess!" he says, "something has to be decided upon: either you travel with the Count, in which case we say our fond farewells for ever, or, Maria, you stay here!"

"Stay here? But don't you know, Viktor, what that will mean?"

"I do know," he replied: "that will mean that you break off all ties with your husband."

"And are you not afraid for me? Are you not afraid, either of society's opinion or, perhaps, of my pangs of conscience? You egoist!…"

The Countess began to sob… But the young man was implacable. On his face, as always, was to be seen neither a smile nor pity. He was calm, as at a duel, when a man's fate will be decided within a minute.

"Society's opinion!" he said cold-bloodedly. "Society doesn't interfere in what does not offend it. It doesn't see what is kept from it; it likes openness in life and is inquisitive only as regards secrets; then society starts to find things out – and woe betide that woman about whom there's nothing to say! Society gets cross and punishes an innocent woman with slander… You need to be decisive in life, to choose one role or another. Either be the victim of a hundred idiots in gold spectacles who will slander you only to interest their lady during dances, or just say to society: 'I despise you, I'm not afraid of your gossip, I shall act as my feelings tell me to' – and then society quietens down, like a lamb. It seems to fear a woman who knows how to despise it! So, choose, Countess…"

The Countess remained silent.

"Is there really not a possibility," she said finally, "of reconciling these two extremes? I understand that for you to live in the same city with me is impossible; but I should write to you every day; you can travel out to visit us…"

"And you call me an egoist, Maria? What? For me again to have to keep up with your husband, to catch his idiocies on the wing, to make wise sense out of them and present them to him as compliments? And with this shabby flattery purchase the happiness of seeing you occasionally, mixed half-and-half with the risk? No, Maria, life is short; even without that, it is full of bitterness. Why go looking for suffering when, with one decisive word, it is possible to secure one's happiness? Do you yourself not every minute curse the day of your marriage, are you not every minute afraid that some unexpected thing will not put a stop to our meetings?..."

"All that is as you say," replied Maria, "but conscience, conscience! You have forgotten about that."

Vorotynsky flared up, but his face did not even redden; he coolly picked up his hat and, with a smile, said:

"As far as conscience is concerned, then for that problem I advise you to ask an explanation of his highness, who is so hard-hearted that he deprives our stage of one of its best dancers."

With these words he wanted to leave. The Countess grabbed him by the arm:

"What are you saying, Viktor?"

"You know," he replied, "that I always speak the truth, and to everyone, apart from your husband, whenever I assure him that he is extremely witty. Madame *** is setting off, if not with you, tender pair, then at least straight after you."

Maria threw herself into her armchair; Vorotynsky withdrew.

One day Akinfy Vasilyevich, very anxious, went into the study of the young Count, who was encircled by suitcases, boxes and everything required for the road.

"What does this mean?" said Akinfy Vasilyevich: "Are you leaving your wife here?"

"She wants that herself," replied the Count with some embarrassment. "What is more, my dearest Uncle, I must confess to you that, for both of us, a parting will be useful; of course, just for a certain time."

"I don't understand you..."

"You see, Uncle," the Count continued, "I am ashamed to tell you, but we have both been worried by these strange letters, in which an unknown person threatens us with disaster, if we remain together: you know how dangerous secret enemies can be…"

"Who is it, this one?" cried out Uncle.

"The Black Glove."

"The Black Glove? My God! Don't you know that this Black Glove was none other than I?"

"What? You?" exclaimed the young man.

"Yes, my friend. I considered it necessary to employ this small deception. When you got married, I was afraid of one thing: that you would be too happy; and as perfect happiness is contrary to nature, I was afraid that your happiness would quickly bore you. I sought out a means so as to bring upon you a small anxiety, which would make you fear for one another, and more tightly strengthen the tie between you."

The young Count could hardly keep himself from laughing. Akinfy Vasilyevich went on:

"At that time I was persuaded to read a novel by Walter Scott, in fact *Redgauntlet.** One scene in that, where a girl from the Jacobite party throws a glove to one of the English King's knights, gave me the idea of throwing a glove into your bedroom with a letter I made up. Now you can see that there is no reason for your wife to remain here."

"Thank you, Uncle: you have delivered us from great anxiety; but, all the same, it is not possible for the Countess to move away with me. Have you noticed how her health has deteriorated?"

"No, I haven't noticed that."

"Oh, how is that!" the Count retorted. "She is always getting a bit faint, and the doctors have definitely said that any move would be harmful to her."

"Going to dances, apart," Uncle sadly remarked.

"Yes… dances," said the Count, "for amusement. But just imagine the long journey, the bad roads. If we had here, just like in England, surfaced roads everywhere, that would be a different matter... You do understand?"

"I understand, I understand entirely," replied the old fellow sadly.

He clearly saw that all his plans for the happiness of his charges had been shattered, but was not able to reproach himself for anything. He had secured their estate, supplied them with wealth, consolidated their bodily health, painstakingly preserved them from all the upsurges of what he regarded as imagination, from everything that could bring into motion intellect and sensibility. There was no way that he could explain to himself how he had not succeeded in his systematization in the *practical* rules for a basic upbringing.

So how did this all end? Akinfy Vasilyevich went off to the country to busy himself with estate management and to get carried away by nature. The Count went off to *** to take up his position – and not unaccompanied. The Countess remained in Petersburg.

THE APPARITION

1838

Dedicated to Nikolai Vasilyevich Putiata

F OUR OF US WERE seated in the stagecoach: a retired captain,
the head of a service department, Irinei Modestovich and I
myself.* The first two stood rather on ceremony, letting out various courtesies one to the other, occasionally starting a slight
argument, but soon cutting that short. Irinei Modestovich
talked away unceasingly; everything, a carriage passing by, a
pedestrian, some bit of a village, everything provided him with
cause for conversation. Taking it for granted that his audience
could not jump away from him out of the stagecoach, it was
lucky that he kept relating tale after tale, in which, of course,
house-sprites, devils and apparitions had a leading role. I
could not but cogitate as to where he had picked up such a
quantity of demonism, and I dozed away most peaceably
under the babbling of his squeaky voice. My other companions
were listening away to him from nothing better to do, but not
without paying some attention – and that was quite sufficient
for Irinei Modestovich.

"What castle would that be?" asked the retired captain,
looking out of the window. "You surely know some peculiar
story regarding it, too," he added, turning towards Irinei
Modestovich.

"I do know about it," answered Irinei Modestovich, "the
identical story that can be related regarding many of the houses
of nowadays: that is to say that people have lived, eaten, drunk
and died in it. But this castle does remind me of an anecdote in

69

which just such a castle plays an important role. Imagine just that all that I shall now relate to you took place beneath these very collapsing vaults. Anyway, it's all the same thing, so long as there is belief in the narrator. All travellers tell their stories in this way, for the most part; only they don't have my candour.

"In my younger days I would often call in at the house of my neighbour, a highly amiable lady... Don't get the idea that anything improper was going on: my neighbour had already reached such years at which a woman will herself acknowledge that time has passed her by. She had neither daughters nor nieces. Her house was like all the houses of *** region: three or four rooms, a dozen or so armchairs, the same number of other chairs, a couple of lamps in the dining room, a pair of candles in the drawing room... But I don't know: there was something in the mien of this woman, in her completely ordinary words, I think, even something about her mahogany table covered with an oilcloth, or coming from within the walls of her house – something or other, every evening, that would whisper in your ears: off you go this evening to Maria Sergeyevna's. And this was experienced not only by me; through the long winter evenings unexpected guests would gather, just as though this had all been arranged beforehand. Our occupations there were the most usual: we drank tea and played Boston; sometimes we leafed through journals; but all of this was more enjoyable to do at Maria Sergeyevna's than in other houses – and this we ourselves found very strange. The whole thing, as I now suspect, came down to Maria Sergeyevna not inflicting on anyone details of lawsuits or domestic business; she didn't care for scandal, didn't communicate to anyone her observations about goings on in the locality, or the behaviour of her servants. She didn't try to draw out of you what you wanted to conceal; she didn't strew you with endearments to your face, nor did she have a laugh at you when you had left; she didn't get cross when someone didn't appear in her drawing room for an entire six

months, or even forgot her name day or birthday. She had
not a single one of the pretensions or the whims that make
the society of the ladies of *** region so intolerable. She was
neither sanctimonious nor superstitious; she didn't require
you to think in a particular way or to speak about any particular thing; she would not be outraged when you were of
the opposite opinion to her; she didn't request from you any
donations. She didn't sit you forcibly down for cards or the
piano – she had her grasp of tolerance in its fullest sense. In
her drawing room, any decent person could do, think and
say everything they wished. In brief, a good tone dominated
her house, one which was rare in the society of *** region,
and the essentiality of which is even to this day understood
by very few. I myself have keenly appreciated the difference
between the bearing and lifestyle of Maria Sergeyevna and
that of other women, but have been incapable of conveying
my impression in a nutshell."

"Allow me to stop you here," said the head of department.
"What do you mean? As though a good tone consists in the
hostess not engaging with her guests? No, forgive me, we
ourselves frequent the very best company... I must argue with
you here. How could this be so? How can it be?"

"It is said," replied Irinei Modestovich, "that the simpler
the hostess's manner, the more at ease and restful it is for the
guests, and that a man accustomed to good society is always
recognizable from the simplicity of his manner."

"And I am of that opinion," added the retired captain. "I
can't put up with all this preciousness! It used to be that, at our
Brigadier General's evenings, you couldn't unbutton your coat
or move an inch: it was oh so stiff! It's quite another matter
when you are off out with one of your own: then it's uniform
off, a bottle of rum on the table, and you're away with it!"

"No, have it your own way," the head of department retorted,
"I cannot agree with you. What is all this simplicity? Simplicity!

Your own home is good enough for simplicity. But in the social world it's pleasing to show off one's bearing, one's capability for mixing, for weighing every word on the scales, so that in each of our words it should be apparent that one is not totally ignorant, but well brought up..."

Irinei Modestovich found himself in complete bewilderment between these two opposite poles and was thinking up a means of how not to land himself either in a boozy chit-chat or into the company of the impeccable gentleman. Noting my friend's discomposure, I intervened in the conversation.

"However, the way we are going," I said, "we'll never reach the end of our story. Now, at what point had you stopped, Irinei Modestovich?"

Our adversaries went silent, since both of them were pleased with themselves. The head of department felt sure that he had trampled all of my friend's considerations into the dust; whereas the captain felt that Irinei Modestovich was of the same opinion as himself.

Irinei Modestovich continued:

"I, seemingly, had told you that we, ourselves not knowing exactly how, would gather each evening at Maria Sergeyevna's, without having arranged it in advance. It has to be acknowledged, however, that such improvisations, like all improvisations in society, did not always succeed for us. At times there would turn up those from whom a pair would play only whist, and two others only Boston; some who would play for high stakes and some for low – and so card parties couldn't be made up.

"This occurred on one occasion, as I now remember, in deep autumn. Rain with hoar frost was pouring down in torrents, streaming along the pavements in rivers, and the wind was blowing out the lamps. In the drawing room, apart from me, sat about four people, in anticipation of their partners. But these partners had seemingly been put off by the weather, and so we, in the meantime, engaged ourselves in conversation.

"The conversation, as is often the case, moving from subject to subject, stopped on the topic of presentiments and visions."

"I was just waiting for that!" exclaimed the head of department. "He'll never get by without apparitions…"

"That's no wonder!" retorted Irinei Modestovich, "these topics usually attract common attention. The mind we possess, worn out by our prosaic life, will be involuntarily attracted by these mysterious happenings which form the popular poetry of our society and serve to prove that from poetry, as from original sin, no one in this life can escape."

The esteemed functionary nodded his head significantly, wishing to display that he had thoroughly absorbed the import of these words. Irinei Modestovich continued:

"All the most likely happenings of this type, familiar to us, had already been related in turn: those about people turning up after death, about faces which peer in at you from second-floor windows, about dancing stools, and other such goings on.

"One of the gathering, throughout the entire narrative sequence, had preserved a deep silence, and just smiled slyly whenever we vociferated in horror. This gentleman, already getting on quite a bit in years, was an incorrigible Voltairean from the last century. Quite often in our debates, without joking, he would conclude his argument with some verse or other from *Épître à Uranie* or from the *Discours en vers* by Voltaire* and would be surprised when, even after that, we should dare not to agree with him. His favourite saying was: 'I believe only that twice two makes four'.

"When our entire arsenal of stories had been exhausted, we addressed to this gentleman a somewhat derisory request to relate to us himself something or other in the same vein. He had guessed our intention, and he responded:

"'You know that I cannot endure all these ravings. I take after my father in this. An apparition once got the idea of appearing before him – an apparition with all the right qualities: a pale face, a melancholy look; but my late lamented papa stuck his tongue out at it, at which the apparition was so astounded that, in consequence, it never again dared to make an appearance – neither to him, nor to anyone from our family. I now follow Dad's method whenever, in the journals, I bump into a romantic tale from one of your modish storytellers. Only I have noticed that they are far more shameless than the apparitions, and never cease ramming themselves down my throat, notwithstanding all the faces I pull at them. But don't go thinking, though, that I can't also relate a horror story. Just listen to this. I shall tell you a true story; and I'll wager that your hair will stand on end.

"'About thirty years ago – I had only just entered the military service then – our regiment had stopped in a particular locality; we were part of the reserve. Rumours were going round that the campaign was ending, and these rumours were corroborated by our not being disturbed in that spot for over a month. This period of time is quite sufficient for military personnel to get to know the local population. I put up in the home of a certain well-to-do female landowner, a really nice cheerful woman with a lot to say. We became really chummy. Almost every evening, guests would visit her, just like coming here, and we would spend a really pleasant time. About a kilometre from this spot, on slightly higher ground, was to be found an ancient castle, with its windows in half-circles, its little towers with whirligig features. In short, it had all the fancy pieces of the so-called Gothic architecture, which then got laughed at, but which, with the present decline in taste, are getting back again into fashion. At that time, this would never have entered our heads. We just regarded this castle as a distortion, which indeed it was, likening it first to a barn, then to a pigeon loft, then to a pâté of some sort, or then to a lunatic asylum. 'Who is the owner of that confectionery pie?' I once asked my hostess.

"'"My friend, the Countess," she replied. "She is a charming lady; you really should make her acquaintance... Countess Malvina was very unhappy previously," my hostess went on, "she had had a lot to bear in her time. In her younger days she fell in love with one young man, but he was poorly off, although he was a Count, and her parents just would not give her to him in marriage. But the Countess was of an ardent disposition. She was passionately in love with the young man, and finally she not only ran away from home with him, but married him, too – and that, in my view, was completely superfluous. You can imagine how much of a row this occurrence caused. The Countess's mother was a woman of the strictest disposition, from the old days, proud of her distinguished origins, haughty, surrounded by a bunch of flatterers, and used, for the whole of her life, to blind submission from everyone around her. Malvina's dashing off was a heavy blow for her; for one thing, the insubordination of her own daughter enraged her; for another, she saw in this deed an eternal stain upon her family. The poor young Countess, knowing her mother's disposition, for a long time did not dare to show herself before her; her letters remained unanswered; and she was in absolute despair. Nothing comforted her: neither the love of her husband, nor the assurances of her friends that her mother's rage could not be carried on for much longer, particularly now that things were wrapped up. Thus passed six months of continuous sufferings. I frequently saw her at that time – she was completely unlike herself. She eventually became pregnant; her distress intensified. A woman's nerves at this time usually play an important role: they are felt as though more alive; every single thought and every word are a thousand times more alarming than before. The idea of giving birth beneath her mother's anger became intolerable for Malvina. The thought of it smothered her, prevented her from sleeping, and exhausted all her strength. Finally, she couldn't contain herself. 'Whatever becomes of it,' she said, 'I'm going to throw myself at Mother's feet.' To no avail, we wanted to stop her; to no avail, we counselled her to await the birth and then, together with the baby, appear before the riled Countess; to no avail, we told her that glimpsing an innocent child affects, more than anything, even the most callous hearts – but our words were to no effect. Faint-heartedness won out, and one morning, when all were still asleep, the unhappy Countess left her house on the sly and made off to the castle, bursting into the bedroom, where her mother still lay in bed, and threw herself down on her knees.

"'"The old Countess was an odd woman; she belonged to the category of those beings difficult to fathom. It is never possible to recognize what they want, and for they themselves, perhaps, this is even harder. Her mental disposition was played upon by everything around her: a trivial word, a letter received, or the weather. She might get either delighted or distressed through identical causes, in accordance with whatever minor circumstances prevailed.

"'"The first reaction that her daughter produced on the Countess was one of fright. Half awake, she could not imagine who this woman was, in a white dress, sobbing and grabbing her by the knees and pulling the blanket from her. At first she took her daughter for a ghost, then for a madwoman, and finally her fright changed into annoyance. Her daughter's tears did not move her; her condition did not move her; maternal instinct did not touch her – egoism won the day. 'Clear off!' she yelled. 'I don't know you: I curse you!...' Poor Malvina almost lost consciousness, but her own maternal instinct did reinforce her. With some effort, but with a certain expressiveness, she articulated in a broken voice: 'Curse me... but do have mercy on my child.' 'I do curse you,' repeated the enraged Countess, ' – and your child! May it be your death sentence!' The hapless Malvina fell to the floor in a dead faint.

"'"This fainting fit produced a stronger effect on the old Countess than all her daughter's words. Once more the Countess was scared stiff. Her capricious nerves could not tolerate the sight of this. She nimbly leapt from her bed, rang her bell, sent for the doctor and when her unhappy daughter regained consciousness, she was already in the embraces of her mother. All was forgiven, and forgotten...

""From then on, Malvina with her husband were installed in the castle. She soon gave birth to a son. The old Countess, quite ashamed of her reprehensible conduct, it seemed, made it her aim in life to comfort her daughter by all means open to a human being. On a few occasions she solemnly forswore her curse, wrote her retraction down on paper and made her daughter carry this around herself in a locket. The young Countess wore it all the time. Her son grew up and entered the service. But even to this time, the old Countess considered herself indebted to her daughter and attempted to gratify her like a child. Her riches allowed her all the resources required for this. It seems as though fate itself was trying to expiate the old Countess's conduct. Quite recently they had been awarded several millions in a lawsuit. This gave them the means to embellish their castle with all the caprices of luxury. What wouldn't you be able to find there? There's an English garden, and a wondrous grand table, and a wine cellar full of hundred-year-old Hungarian, and fountains of cold and hot water, and marble floors and winter gardens – in a word, it's paradise! The balls and evening gatherings never cease. If you wish, I'll introduce you to the Countess: you will be received with delight."'

"What could have been more pleasurable than this suggestion to young officers, for whom, for a whole six months, all the world's pleasures had been reduced to fraternal boozing in a village hut?"

"We could do worse than that!" remarked the captain, stroking his moustache.

"'The next day we started off to meet the Countess. We were introduced to her by our hostess and had occasion to be satisfied that she had not deceived us. The establishment was set up in a veritable lordly style. Each one of us was led into a separate room, in which there was everything that could be thought of for life's comforts. There was an excellent feather bed, which, after straw, seemed a marvel to us. Each room had a bath with hot and cold taps; all the fancies of toiletry. There were servants, who tiptoed about and could guess one's slightest need. Every day there was a stupendous dinner, with stupendous wines.

"'The old Countess, who no longer raised herself from her armchair, was still amiable, and the so-called young Countess, although she was now past forty, was as fresh, active and fidgety as a fifteen-year-old girl. Many of us counted it our duty to pass her our military endearments, and others fell for her, head over heels. Her husband shut his eyes at this and, seemingly, even was glad that his wife had the occasion to flirt and excite the passions of young officers. A habit for pleasures and incessant diversion was the essential in the lifestyle in this house. Just one demand was made upon us: to eat and drink all day and to dance all night until we dropped. We lived on the fat of the land. Within a few days, the joyfulness and the amusement in the house increased twofold. The son of the young Countess arrived home on leave – a splendid, jovial young chap. He too, like us, had long been rambling round village huts and, with the full voracity of youth, abandoned himself to the pleasures presented to him by his home roof and a merry family circle.

"'The day of our going away had been fixed, and our hosts wanted to entertain us to a final splendid ball. Invited were the neighbours, male and female, from all the places around; they proposed illuminating the garden and indulging in a wonderful firework display. The evening before, in the middle of discussions concerning the following day (for, almost like family members, we took part in all the domestic busying about) a conversation got going, just like now, about ghosts. The young Countess recollected there being one room in the castle which, from some considerable time past, enjoyed the privilege of frightening all residents of the locality with a variety of horrible sounds and apparitions. This very room, through a shortage of space, was being occupied by the Countess's son. He affirmed, with a laugh, that up until now house-sprites had had on him just one effect: they had forced upon him really deep sleep. We laughed about this with him, and then went off to our own rooms.

"'On the next day a considerable number of people arrived at the castle. Dancing began almost from ten in the morning, and we danced right up to dinner, and after dinner, right up to midnight. None of us even thought about having to mount our horses at five the next morning. But, to tell the truth, by the evening's end, we were worn out to an extreme, and were quite pleased to notice that, towards one, the guests were beginning to depart. The rooms were getting empty; we also wanted to go off to our bedrooms; but the young Countess, to whom a twenty-four hour dance was equivalent to taking a glass of water, zealously begged us to keep on asking the ladies to waltz, in order to delay the leavers. We exhausted the last of our energy, and finally had to ask permission of the Countess to retire, alluding to her son, who had long since gone off to his room.

"'"Oh," said the Countess, "why should you follow that lazy-bones's example! We should teach him a lesson for his sloth. How can he go off to his bed when there are so many pretty ladies still in the dance hall! Just follow me!"

"'The young man was sleeping that agitated type of sleep to be expected after a day spent in ceaseless movement. The squeak of the door woke him. But what a shock it was for him when, by the pallid light of the nocturnal icon-lamp, he sighted a row of white apparitions, coming closer to his bed! Still half asleep, he snatched up his pistol and shouted: "Get away, I'll shoot!" But the apparition at the forefront carried on approaching his bed and, seemingly, wanted to grab hold of him with outstretched hands. Perhaps in fright, or from still not being properly awake, the young man cocked the gun and a shot rang out...

"'"Aah! I forgot to wear Mother's locket!" screamed Malvina as she sank to the floor. We all, dressed up like ghosts, rushed over to her and lifted her sheet... Her face was so white that it was impossible to recognize her: she had been mortally wounded. At that minute the far-off banging of a drum let us know that our regiment was taking to the field. We left behind the sorrowful house, in which we had spent such pleasant days. Since then I don't know how it all ended; but at least, even if I have never seen an apparition, I have been an apparition myself – and that is surely worth something. All ghost stories are something of this type. I dare say they've fabricated God knows what out of this; but it was quite a simple matter really, as you can see.' And the storyteller gave out a laugh.

"At this juncture, a certain young man, who had listened to the entire story with great attention, went up to him. 'It is with great accuracy,' he said, 'that you have narrated this occurrence. I know about it, for I belong myself to the family to whom it happened. But one thing is unknown to you: namely, that the Countess is in fine fettle to this day and that it was not she who led you into the room of her son, but indeed some sort of an apparition, which still makes appearances in the castle.'

"The storyteller went pale. The young man went on: 'There was a lot of talk about this event, but there was nothing that ever explained it. The remarkable thing is just that all those who told the story of this incident died within two weeks of relating it.' Having said his piece, the young man picked up his hat and left the room.

"The storyteller paled even more. The assured, cold tone of this young man, clearly, had struck him. I must confess that we all shared this feeling with him and could not but fall silent.

Then we wanted to talk about something else, but with no success, and we soon dispersed to our respective homes. A few days later we learned that our apparition-scoffer had fallen ill, and indeed very seriously. To his physical sufferings were added the ravings of his imagination. He ceaselessly conjured up a pale woman in a white shawl, who kept pulling him from his bed. And just imagine," Irinei Modestovich added in a tragic voice, "within two weeks exactly, there was one guest less in Maria Sergeyevna's drawing room."

"How strange!" remarked the captain, "how very strange!"

The head of department, as a man from Petersburg, accustomed to not being surprised by anything, had listened through the whole tale with the air of an official reading a clerical dispatch on the provision of fixed-term lists.

"There's nothing surprising in this," he said in an arrogant voice, "a lot of things happen to a person through his mentality, yes – their mentality. Just as I had a clerk once, seemingly a decent enough chap, who was always asking for a full position. To get him off my back, I put him on to putting the old archives in order, saying there would be a position for him when he'd got the archive straight. But he, the poor blighter, totally shackled himself to it. A year went by, and then a second year – day and night he rooted about in the archive. I finally took mercy on him and was just intending to recommend him to the director, when they suddenly came to me, saying that something bad had happened to my archivist. I went off to the room where he worked – and he wasn't there. I looked around: he had climbed on to the very top shelf, had squatted down up there between the stacks of paperwork, just holding in his hands a whack of it.

"'What's wrong with you?' I shouted to him. 'Come down here!' What do you think he replied? 'I can't, Ivan Grigorich, I can't at all: I'm a settled case!'"

And the head of department guffawed away. Tears welled up in Irinei Modestovich's eyes. "Your story," he muttered, "is sadder than mine."

The captain, who hadn't paid much attention to the civil service story, was seemingly puzzling away over the apparition tale and finally, as though regaining his senses, he asked Irinei Modestovich:

"What, then: at this Maria Sergeyevna's of yours, were they drinking punch?"

"No," answered Irinei Modestovich.

"That's odd!" the captain muttered. "Very odd!"

Meanwhile the stagecoach came to a stop; and we descended.

"Really, though, did that storyteller indeed die?" I asked.

"I never said he did," Irinei Modestovich replied swiftly in his thinnest voice, smiling and giving a little jump, as was his wont.

THE WITNESS

1839

(dedicated to A.I. Koshelyov)

I JUMPED OUT OF MY CARRIAGE and kissed my native soil. ... The sound of a Russian Orthodox Church bell recalled me from that feeling of self-oblivion which overcomes the soul at the sight of the fatherland, specially after a separation from it of ten years. Not too far away, on a hillock, the walls of a monastery shone white. My tiredness forgotten, I rushed to the open gates of the place of worship, not with the cool curiosity of a traveller, but just as the infant rushes to the maternal embrace. This is everyone's experience, following a lengthy separation from the motherland.

Vespers had gone. Through the semicircular windows came the drawn-out, crimson rays of the setting sun, playing in the clouds of church incense, settling in tiers on the gleaming gilt of the iconostasis – like a long, bitter prayer, stirred up by bloody passions, finally getting through to the awning surrounding the testament of the soul. The fresh evening air was percolating through the opened doors. Villagers were starting to leave the church; after them, in a black stream, stretched the monastic brethren. I remained stationary; the deserted church seemed to me even more majestic, even more auspicious. Its appearance promoted the kind of thoughts that disappear amidst a crowd, in the middle of stormy life, and which cannot be caught in words, but which speak so distinctly to the heart. An almost inaudible rustle made me aware that I was not alone. In a distant corner I noticed a monk stretched out on a cold platform. An involuntary curiosity compelled me also to stay in the church. Eventually the recluse stood up; his face lit up in the rays of the sun.

The unknown figure seemed to recognize me as well. We came closer.

"Is that you, Rostislav?"

"Is that you, Grigory?" and we clasped each other around the neck. I recognized my old friend from active service, my old boyhood friend.

"What does that garb signify? What is the meaning of your pale, exhausted face? Is that you, the bold hussar, the star of the Petersburg balls?"

The monk did not answer a word, but sighed deeply and led me to his cell. This is what he told me:

"Shortly after your departure to other lands I went off on leave to see my family. At home I found my mother, who was already very weak and ill. I barely recognized my younger brother: at his age, a person changes so quickly – and I hadn't seen him for five years. He was now about seventeen; he was a good-looking boy and was of a very pleasant youthful disposition. Mother didn't want to let go of him. He was the one child of hers that she had fed herself, and you know how that relationship can produce between mother and child some sort of a mysterious, indissoluble, almost physical bond, which strengthens in the highest degree what is in any case a fervent maternal feeling, and does not disappear with the years. Vyacheslav would have acceded completely to his mother's wishes. But once he had seen my splendid uniform, my moustache, and heard the stories about my regimental friends, the theatre, and all the enjoyments of Petersburg life – he forgot about his mother's wishes and his promises, and he began persistently asking her for permission to enter military service. To his entreaties I added my own. I described to our mother all the advantages that this way of life would bring him. I reminded her that we would each be there in support of the other; I promised that I would be permanently close to Vyacheslav, to be for him not only a brother, but a father. After a drawn-out tussle, she called me over alone to her couch and said to me:

"'I am no longer able to resist your supplications. I do not wish for my children ever to be able to accuse me of preventing their happiness in life. Take Vyacheslav with you. But, Rostislav, do not rejoice in my consent. You cannot comprehend the responsibility I am imposing on you. If I were able to get from this couch to the carriage, I would travel with you, but that would do no good. To me, in my state, it's all the same, whether it's seven hundred kilometres or seventeen metres: there's no way I would keep up with you. I would only be a hindrance to you in life, and you know that I do not belong to that category of mothers who, through some form of egoism, love to keep their children tied to them by a leash, knowing full well how utterly bored they are. Now, just listen: Vyacheslav is an infant. He doesn't know himself what he wants, he doesn't know people, or life. But you, Rostislav, you are no longer a child. You have got through that stage of awful crisis when a person doesn't have in the head a single thought of his own, when one cannot really be aware of anything, when any word spoken louder than the last one may lead one away from the straight and narrow. Naturally, you will have a strong influence on your brother. For a long time yet he will be thinking with your head, feeling with your heart, and living through your life. Take care of yourself, and take care of him. I won't accept from you any excuses – for whatever he does, you will be responsible to me. In your dealings with your brother you must foresee everything, warn him of everything, and you will be answerable to me for his behaviour – both in this life, and in the next.'

"These words are still sounding in my ears even now. Mother was deeply moved – and I was as well. In my heart I was firmly convinced that her trust in me was not at all misplaced, and I took a harrowing oath that I would fulfil her sacred bidding.

"The end of my leave was approaching, and we pulled ourselves away from our mother's embraces. I had to get Vyacheslav into the carriage almost unconscious: he was crying like a child.

"I am not going to describe to you the first years of our Petersburg life. I could not complain about Vyacheslav. He was a bit frivolous, but still maintained a completely chaste soul, such a rare thing these days among young people. Trifling things upset him; and trifles amused him. He was all on the surface, saying anything that came into his head. At a happy moment he would jump on to tables and chairs; at a sad time he could not hold back the tears. Sometimes, for hours at a time, he would run around the room with Boxen, his young setter; and then he would say that they loved each other for being of the same character, for the one was just as mad as the other. And indeed, Boxen, who wouldn't even let me near him, allowed Vyacheslav to do everything with him that entered his empty head; and when, as used to happen, they got carried away by their playing, I had to summon up all my composure so as not to burst out laughing, or to get really angry. But, I must confess, I preferred my brother's childish simplicity to the premature guardedness of some of his comrades, who, it seemed, must have been diplomats in their cradles. I introduced him to quite a number of ladies; and I took him to balls. He danced diligently, with full and open enjoyment. His cheerful and transparent appearance could not help but please: the ladies ran after him without mercy, taking him for a complete child, and he, the prankster, as they say *faisait le gros dos.** I took a pride in him, watching him at it, like a father watching his infant.

"Eventually the long and impatiently awaited day arrived: Vyacheslav was commissioned with the rank of cornet. To imagine his joy is impossible. Unfamiliar with the decorous pretence of today's young men, he twirled himself unceasingly in front of the mirror, first to this side and then to that, in order

the better to be able to see his epaulettes. Then he rushed over
to embrace me, then he put on his three-cornered hat; then he
dragged Boxen around by the paws. 'Do you know, Boxen,'
he said, 'that I am now a cornet? Do you understand that? Do
you realize that now you'll be walking along Nevsky Prospect
with me, with your master, the cornet?...' And it did seem as
though Boxen understood him; at least he wagged his tail and
answered Vyacheslav's words with a loud bark. All these simple
incidences in our then life, all these words of Vyacheslav's, are
so alive in my memory."

Tears rolled down from the recluse's eyelashes. He took a
deep breath, and then seemed engrossed, probably trying to
gather his thoughts; eventually he went on:

"One of our comrades, Vetsky, had an elder brother, working
in the Civil Service. I liked him a lot; he was a man of quite
remarkable intelligence, but I don't think I have ever seen a
more awkward man. He had been physically somehow premature and from that suffered from very poor health. He was
fully aware of his physical debility and for that reason permit-
ted himself no excesses – not even any gymnastic exercises.
He walked slowly, taking care with every step. His riding was
such that no horseman could look at him without laughing.
When the younger people pranced around at a fiery gallop, he
would timidly enquire as to which was the most placid horse
and painstakingly examine whether its girth had been properly
strapped. Moreover, he had some sort of a speech impediment,
which gave him a kind of drawl, almost a stammer. You can
imagine the effect he produced in a young crowd of skilled
riders, full of life and dash, often extending to recklessness.

Vetsky was a good companion. He was liked, but everyone
considered it an obligation to make fun of him, of his deli-
cate physique, his inhibitions, and his caution, which often
stretched to timidity. Vetsky tolerated all these taunts with the
greatest composure. Sometimes he would get out of things
with a witty quip, and sometimes he would join in the laugh

at his own expense, but more often he wouldn't know what to reply to unexpected sallies, for it seemed that his mental capabilities could be just as inhibited as his physical ones. He belonged to that category of people easily knocked from their stride if words are slung at them, and who will often be at a complete loss for the first minute or two. But such a position was not a pleasant one for Vetsky, although he tried to cover his anger beneath an ever calm and cool exterior. It was obvious that he was expending every effort not to lose control of himself, repeating with a smile that getting angry made him *unwell*. After a while, I noticed that my brother made fun of Vetsky more than anyone, but we were all so used to laughing at our *tailcoat wearer*, so used to seeing him as an amusing distraction, that I didn't pay special attention to my brother's behaviour. It just seemed so natural to all of us. The thing was, as I found out afterwards, that Vyacheslav became jealous of Vetsky over a certain beauty who, through some strange caprice, preferred our awkward eccentric to my skilful, handsome horseman.

"New officers had to, as they say, *wet their epaulettes*. They took days sorting it all out, so as to organize a bash, first for one of them, then for another, but the rapid exodus of the regiments from barracks into the Petersburg environs compelled them to postpone their binges until such time as they would have moved completely into summer quarters. Finally the bingeing days began. You cannot have any conception of these. Ten years is an entire age in Russia. Gone are the days of the crude, unbridled orgies, which you can still remember. Young people now are in their senses, even after a bottle of wine. Today's orgies are orderly, respectable ones. A woman can attend them without blushing. But, despite that, as of old, champagne still has its effect on people, and blood will still go to the head from it. It may be true that now, they say, it's no longer a matter of honour to drink oneself under the table, but, in the old way, from wine a man becomes merrier, quicker, more unpredictable in his moves and, in the old way, all his feelings become keener. Every thought, otherwise lying forgotten deep in the soul in a sober state, will magnify under a soaking of champagne, as though under a microscope.

"This spree took place in a fairly small wooden country house. They didn't stint on the champagne. Moreover, this spree was not the first one, and everyone's head, even that of Vetsky, was, as they used to say, at least half-cocked. It got to two o'clock in the morning. I felt suffocated, so I left the villa, and walked off around the countryside. As I now recall it, the night was a cool and bright one. With delight I drank in the fresh air, and admired the village view, which was already beginning to glow crimson from the first rays of dawn. It was quiet all round, but just one little house was lit up – the one with the feasting going on. Shadows scuttled across the windows; guffaws and the merry shouts of young people reached me.

"Suddenly... everything went quiet. I unwittingly shuddered at this sudden silence. My heart started beating strongly, just as though I had just heard some dreadfully bad news. Without being aware of my feelings, I involuntarily doubled my step on my way back to the villa. When I walked in, my foreboding proved justified. Inside the doorway I ran straight into Vetsky, a sword in his hands. He didn't say a word to me, but was as white as a sheet, and was anxious to conceal an inner agitation under his indifferent smile.

"I was told straight away what had happened in my absence: a frivolous, childish prank, but one which had to have a bloody end...

"The young people had opened the window on to the yard. One of them took it into his head to jump out from it, and then another, and then a third one. Anyone falling would hurt himself, because the window was quite a high one. Amid general laughter, the risk aroused in the young folk a strange sense of self-esteem: everyone wanted to give it a try – would anyone break his neck in the course of this exploit?

"'Well, how about you, then?' – my brother had said to the older Vetsky, with a mocking smile.

"'I am not intending to jump,' Vetsky replied coldly.

"'That's no good! You've really got to jump.'

"'I told you, I don't want to.'

"'You don't want to jump,' my brother replied, flushed with wine, 'because you're a coward.'

"'I wouldn't advise you to repeat those words,' said Vetsky.

"My poor brother himself didn't remember what he said, or what he did.

"'Not only will I repeat them,' he retorted, hands on hips, 'but I shall make a point of telling Countess M—' (the lady that both were running after), 'I shall say to her: "Your tender admirer, he's a coward!" Do you want to bet I don't?'

"Vetsky, notwithstanding all his capacity for composure, completely lost his temper. He grabbed my brother roughly by the arm and muttered:

"'Just you dare, you lunatic!'

"A blow with a glove across the face was the reply.

"What now was to be done? For a time I thought about reconciling the opponents, but how? Forcing my brother to apologize would be impossible: his pride had been inflamed by his officer's uniform. He realized himself that he had acted stupidly, but to begin his career with what he would have called an unworthy trick, to get cold feet – to this he would not agree. I myself at that time could not envisage this other than with horror. It remained for me to work on Vetsky. I was counting on his constant timidity, on his constant caution and good sense. At that moment of egoism, it seemed to me that it would cost nothing to leave this man under a yoke of universal scorn, just in order to save my brother. Restraining my own sense of pride, I went off to see our tailcoated civil servant.

"When I entered his room, he was sitting at his writing table and calmly smoking a cigar. His composure alarmed me.

"'I wanted to speak,' I said to him, 'not with your second, but with you. You, as an intelligent man, must really see in my brother's behaviour nothing other than the prank of a mere boy, who doesn't merit your attention.'

"Vetsky gave me a look of surprise and replied with a smile.

"'You can believe,' he said, 'that I, more than anyone, regret your brother's behaviour. But allow me to say to you: you yourself are not thinking about what you're saying: just tell me this – can this really be left without attention?'

"These few words changed my way of thinking about Vetsky. I wanted to touch his inner feelings. I related to him all our family circumstances – our farewell to Mother, her words... I made no effort to spare Vyacheslav, calling him a crazy, retarded child; I even uttered the word *pardon*.

"'Allow me to ask you,' Vetsky said to me, with his usual cold smile, 'are you offering me an apology in your brother's name, or in your own?'

"I was embarrassed and didn't know what to say to him. He fixed me with a penetrating look.

"'I quite understand your position. I know that your brother will not apologize to me, and that it's not possible for him to apologize to me. I really sympathise with you, and even with him. I am no swashbuckler; duels are not my business. My rule in life has been always to avoid giving cause for any such thing, but,' he added emphatically, 'never to back off, even a step, when danger is unavoidable. Put yourself in my position: how many times have I let go as jokes those sort of words from your brother, which from anyone else would have caused a couple of dozen duels? I spared him for his youth, and I can admit to you, I spared myself, for in life there are quite enough unpleasantnesses without that. And life is short: why sacrifice it over trivialities? But this is a more serious matter. Just think, yourself, what would become of me if, in addition

91

to the generally held opinion about my excessive cautiousness, I should leave the present incident, as you put it, without
attention? You know about society's prejudices: I would find
no quarter anywhere on the globe. Fingers would be pointed
at me. My only recourse would be to shoot myself, but that,
you must agree, would be in contradiction to my *cautiousness*.'

"These words were cold, plain and derisive. In accordance
with my precepts at that time, I could not refute them.

"'If that's the way it is,' I shouted back heatedly, 'then, my
dear sir, you will be having dealings with me.'

"'If that be your pleasure,' replied Vetsky, flicking off the ash
from his cigar, 'but not before we have concluded our dealings
with your little brother. However, you know yourself that,
anyway, your brother, in all probability, would not agree to any
such arrangement. Now, excuse me – I now have a number of
letters to finish.'

"With these words, he made a cold bow. I rushed out of the
room with a feeling of despair in my heart.

"Back in my quarters, Vetsky's second was waiting for me.
He announced that he was charged not to agree to any propos-
als of reconciliation, except the one – that my brother should
agree to apologize to Vetsky before the entire regimental officer
corps. I don't know about now, but certainly then, such a condition seemed completely impossible.

"One last hope remained: Vetsky couldn't shoot. I, in accordance with the precepts of the time, was my brother's natural
second; I was the closest to him and such an undertaking
seemed to me the inevitable duty of kinship and friendship.
Thinking through all the conditions that might give some
advantage to my brother, I proposed that they should fire at
twenty paces, with the first to shoot remaining at the barrier.
I was relying on my brother's marksmanship. Vetsky's second
willingly accepted my proposal. Hardly had we concluded this
homicidal arrangement, when Vyacheslav walked in. Boxen was
jumping about in front of him with a joyful bark. My brother

was trying to display a lack of concern and full composure. He played and jumped about with his dog as always, but I could see that inwardly he was anxious. Probably life was dangling itself before the youth in all its delights. Most certainly he didn't want to part with it. I looked at his fresh and handsome face, and my heart just bled. In those few hours I aged twenty years.

"Within a few minutes we were already at the place. The idea that I had brought my brother to within range of a lead bullet dominated all my capacities for thought and action. In vain did I wish to display the composure required for such occasions – I was quite beside myself. Vetsky's second had to carry out my duties. The decisive minute arrived. I tried to muster all my powers. I inspected Vyacheslav's pistol. They were standing in their places. Vetsky was as cold as ice: a barely noticeable smile was visible on his clenched lips. It was as though he was standing by the fireplace at a dazzling reception. Glancing at Vyacheslav, I noticed with horror that his hand was shaking.

"The signal was given. The opponents slowly began to approach one another... The appearance of danger made Vyacheslav forget all my advice – he fired... Vetsky wobbled, but he did not fall; the bullet had smashed his left shoulder.

"Concealing his pain, he signalled to Vyacheslav to approach the barrier. With an involuntary convulsive movement, my brother obeyed...

"At that moment I froze to the spot; a cold sweat poured down me. I could see the slow approach of Vetsky, his aiming of the murderous cocking piece, and I could see Vetsky's calm, inexorable expression. Now he was just two paces from my brother. I remembered Mother, her words and my promises, and I got into a state close to madness. It all went black, and I lost sense of everything: honour, conscience and the rules of society. I remembered just one thing: that *they were killing my brother right in front of me*... I couldn't bear this instant, and I threw myself at Vyacheslav, grabbed him, shielded him with my own body and shouted to Vetsky:

93

VLADIMIR ODOEVSKY

"'Go on, shoot!'

"Vetsky lowered his pistol.

"'Is that really in the conditions agreed for the duel?' he said, calmly turning to his second.

"A general cry of disapproval resounded from among those present. I was dragged away from my brother... A shot rang out – and Vyacheslav dropped as though dead!

"How can I tell you what was going on with me at that moment? I tore myself away from those holding me, rushed to Vyacheslav and, unconscious of anything, looked at his grievous, dying torments. I saw his eyes closing for ever!... At this same instant, Boxen, on his broken lead, ran up to the bloody spot, landed on Vyacheslav, howled and licked at his wound.

"This sight brought me back to myself. I leaped over, and grabbed at the pistol, but Vetsky, weakened from his wound, was already lying unconscious on a stretcher. Burning for vengeance, I would have thrown myself at the wounded man, ready to tear him to pieces, but the others stopped me... As though through a dream, there rang in my ears reproaches and condemnations from my fellow officers..."

"What more is there to tell you?" the recluse went on. "You know about the consequences of duels. But the punishment for my misdemeanour to me was nothing: my punishment was in my heart. My life was at an end. I wished for only one thing: either to lose my unneeded life in battle with an enemy, or to bury myself alive. I was not favoured with the first honour. Here, far from my native parts, not known to anyone, I am trying through lamentation and sorrow to stifle the voice of my own heart. But to this day dreadful visions awaken me at night... my mother, dying in despair... and in my ears ring the terrible words of the Scripture: 'Cain, where is thy brother?'"

IMBROGLIO

(From the Notes of a Traveller)

1844; Dated 1835

(One of my friends imparted to me this description of a strange adventure, which occurred during his travels around Italy. My friend is not a writer and he is incapable of narrating stylistically and ornately; I am hoping that the interest of the incident in itself will substitute, as far as my readers are concerned, for elegance in the story-telling. I repeat: my friend is not a writer, but just an ordinary traveller, a tourist, who has taken up the pen for the purification of his conscience.)

THE SUN WAS ALREADY SETTING. Our boat was flying like an arrow. The Bay of Naples opened up in all its expanse. Passengers rushed up on deck. Although it was already the seventh day that we had been moving further and further along under the Italian sky, at a view of the shoreline it still seemed to us ever finer. I shall not describe the exclamations, the raptures of our delight: it has to be experienced.

The smoke from the steam boiler, as though angered at its long confinement, leapt forth from the funnel, hissing and spraying. The wheels came to a stop; thousands of little boats surrounded us. Travelling without a servant, I hoisted my little bag on to my shoulder and jumped into one of them.

"*Alle crocelle, a Santa Lucia,*"* I said to the oarsman, having checked in my *Guide de voyageur* which was the very cheapest inn.

"*Sì, signore,*" replied the boatman and flapped away strongly with his oars.

Having got to the inn, I took the first room on offer, tossed my knapsack hurriedly from my shoulders, handed my papers over to the innkeeper and, with all the impatience of a resident of the north, ran out into the street, so as to enjoy the sumptuous Italian night and the majestic scenery appearing before my eyes. For a long time I wandered along the streets and undiscerningly arrived at the *Villa Reale*, on the seashore. Everything struck me, everything riveted my attention – the architecture of the buildings, the clothes that were new to me, and the facial features singed by the sun. I got accustomed to the singing of the fishermen, to the tales of their storytellers; I went into the churches, and peeped in at the little windows of the houses – in short, I delighted fully, as only a person may delight who has suddenly been brought across the sea from the distant north to Tasso's poetic fatherland.

In all this delight, I did not notice the time, as the sky suddenly grew dark. At this point I recalled that twilight doesn't occur in southern countries, and that I, as a foreigner, could easily lose my way; however, other dangers I did not envisage. The time for romantic adventures had passed, even for Italy; the police had suppressed the menacing poetic bandits. At the same time, my modest attire and even more modest purse could not attract any mercenary attention. I thought for a moment and decided to entrust my organism to my local memory – to get to my lodgings without asking anyone. I confess, I almost wanted not to find my inn, so as to have the opportunity of spending the night beneath the open sky. But I didn't have time to cover more than a few steps before I felt two strong arms grabbing me from behind. At the same moment, two other hands threw a kerchief over my face and drew it so tight that I couldn't even cry out, let alone see who had taken it into their heads to divert themselves in this fashion with me.

But it was far from a joke when I could feel my arms and legs being tied, and I was being dragged God knows where with a

considerable rapidity. All resistance was useless. I just allowed
to be done with me all that my abductors felt like doing and
with impatience awaited the upshot of this strange adventure.
Finally we came to a stop. The sound of oars could be heard,
and I soon felt that I must be in a boat. This calmed me slightly.
If I had been snatched by bandits, I thought, then they would
not be standing on quite such ceremony with me. But there
then entered my head stories of people who had been held by
a gang of robbers and could be freed only by means of a large
ransom, pending which the *bravi* turn themselves to cutting
off the noses and ears of their victims. From this thought, a
shudder ran through my limbs: the perception of the wealth
of Russians that they have in Italy; my particularly inadequate
state; the certainty that I could not easily free myself from
these idlers and that, it could well be, a very bitter fate awaited
me. All of this crowded into my head and formed a horrific
picture. But then it came to me that I had never heard tell of
such escapades in Naples, and again I began to lose myself in
conjectures. In vain could I try to listen to my companions'
conversation: they kept a deep silence. Eventually the boat
was tied up to the shore, again my conveyers lifted me in their
arms, taking a few steps – and I heard the squeaking of doors
and felt myself being dragged up some steps. The sounds of
several voices could be heard, getting nearer, nearer. Eventually
a strong hand grabbed me round the chest and a coarse voice,
choking with anger, came out with:

"*Scellerato!*"*

Meanwhile, they untied my legs, dragged me along a few
further steps, and a woman's voice rang out. At that minute,
the band enclosing my face was ripped off and I found myself
in a room covered in black cloth – and, in front of me, an
attractive young woman in a black dress, who threw herself
to embrace me and then suddenly drew back, got down on
her knees and, with a joyful shriek, started to thank God.
Beside me stood a man of elderly years with a naked dagger

in his hand, and another one again, who was also on the grey side.

"It's no good you wanting to deceive us," said the first, in Italian, addressing the young woman, "instead of these scenes, you'd do better to hurry up and say your farewells; his last minute has come."

The young woman made no reply: she looked at me and seemed to be indecisive. Finally, she seemed to pull herself together and shouted:

"Fate has deceived you: this is not he."

At this point I tried to remember the words I had heard in Italian operas and, stumbling at every instant, I said something like the following:

"I see, my dear sirs, that I here am the victim of some sort of misunderstanding and that you take me for another. I won't tell you how contrary it is to honour to seize an unarmed man..."

"Honour is not the question here," the old man exclaimed with anger.

However, my foreign pronunciation, it seemed, did strike home to them; I could see bewilderment on their faces.

"I am a foreigner, my dear sirs," I continued.

"That's a lie!" they both shouted.

"I am only just off the boat."

"We know that."

"I am an officer in the Russian service."

"And that we know, too. We know all your circumstances."

"If that is so, my dear sirs, then I really do not understand why I am here. I have never been in Italy, and I don't even have a single acquaintance here. I am a Russian, my dear sirs, I repeat, and I will add that my government will not tolerate any insult being inflicted upon me..."

My odd phraseology, my foreign pronunciation, evidently made an impression on them. They looked with some indecision first at each other and then at the young woman who, sitting in the armchair, calmly awaited the conclusion of our conversation.

"Will you show us your papers?" one of the strangers said to me.

Now I remembered how careless I had been, leaving my papers with the innkeeper, and not having called first on our envoy. As though having dropped from the sky among people completely unknown to me, in a foreign land, unknown to any of my fellow countrymen, I was completely in the power of my persecutors.

"My papers are still at the inn," I replied. "You can go and check them."

"A great fabrication! You know that we can't go there and check them."

With these words, the stranger unfastened my tailcoat, stuck his hand into the pocket and pulled out from it a note which had remained there by chance from one of my friends, one written in Russian.

"The language this note is written in," I said, "can prove to you that I am not the man you take me for."

"This note doesn't prove anything. We repeat: we know that you have arrived from Russia. Just tell us, if you really are a foreigner, what made you put up anywhere but at the sort of inn where foreigners normally stay? What made you jump out of the boat so hurriedly? What were you running around the streets for? What were you looking into windows for?"

My blood rose, but I tried to conceal my annoyance.

"These questions," I said, "perhaps I ought to answer with a question, too: what right do you have to call me to account? However, in the position in which I find myself, I will tell you that all these apparently strange circumstances are easily explained through the impatience of a traveller from a distant country, one who has landed for the first time in Naples, where, I must confess, he didn't expect any such reception."

"That's all fabrication," shouted the stranger. "We are not children; you can't just pull the wool over our eyes, and you'll soon find this out."

With these words the old man left the room. Several minutes went by in complete silence; my hands were still tied and the younger of the strangers was still standing beside me with a naked dagger. He was watching my every movement. This minute was hard for me; I was panting away from a whole range of feelings stirred up in my heart. If this position had continued for much longer, I could not have borne it and, the unequal strengths not withstanding, would have attempted, even at the cost of my life, to get out of my unprecedented situation. But the door opened and the face, as it seemed to me at least, of an old woman, covered in a shawl, stuck itself round the door.

"That's not him!" she said, taking a look at me and then disappearing.

A shout of anger burst from the chests of the two men; they moved to the side and began quietly to converse between themselves. Little by little their voices rose and, from their words, reflected back from the vault of the room, I was able to conclude that I knew too much for their safety. The good-for-nothings were arguing as to which would be best – to leave me among the living, or to throw me into the sea.

This was a decisive moment, and I said to them:

"It seems that you are now convinced, gentlemen, that I am not the person you had need of. However offensive to me the position that you have placed me in, and however much I might like to demand of you an explanation for your actions against me, I am putting myself in your position. I can give you my word that, if you release me, I shall keep everything that has happened an inviolable secret: it will die along with me."

They looked at me, again went off to the side, and again started arguing.

"I must remind you," I went on, "that for your own benefit it would be much less dangerous to rely on the given word of a man of honour than to conceal this crime through a new crime. I have no interest in finding out your secret and will be leaving Naples in a few days time, as I need hardly say, for good. My death could, sooner or later, lead to the revealing of your secret. My papers have probably already been made known to the police. My compatriots who arrived with me on the boat will demand at the Russian embassy, I can assure you, all possible means for getting to the truth. I leave you to judge which would be more to your advantage."

These words seemed to have some effect on them. They again moved to the side, but their conversation became much calmer. Finally, the younger man came over to me.

"Indeed, my dear sir," he said to me, "we were mistaken. The unusual incident has let you in, to a certain degree, on our family secret. Our own safety would have forced us to resort to the *most reliable* means for the preservation of this secret; but we prefer rather to trust your word of honour. We have decided to release you, dear sir. But you should know that, tied to this event, is the fate of the most distinguished families of Italy; that your slightest indiscretion will immediately be punished with death. What has happened to you today may show you that we have all the necessary means for that. You must swear to all of us, on what to you is the most sacred in life – your motherland, your relatives, your honour – that you will nowhere, ever, in any circumstances, not in confession, not under torture, neither by word nor by gesture: not only not to reveal what has happened to you, but that you will not even attempt to explain it to yourself, nor ever to meet up with any one of us."

There was nothing else to be done – I swore.

"Now you will be free," said the younger man, "you will be taken straight away to your accommodation. But you must forgive us if we shall be compelled to take the earlier precaution of binding up your eyes. Your hands will remain free; we are relying on your nobility, and we trust you will not make the least effort to raise the blindfold."

I allowed them to do everything that they wished.

"From this moment," continued the younger man, "it's as though we never existed, as far as each other is concerned. Try, I advise you for your own benefit, to strip from your memory the very features of our faces. On our behalf, to you, this is a great concession; make sure you value it."

Two strong hands again took me under the armpits, and again we took several steps down the staircase. Again, doors squeaked; again I heard the sound of oars and felt the rocking of a small boat. My guides, as before, were muffled in a deep silence.

Our rowing trip had been underway for quite some time; I was already thinking that the moment of my liberation was getting close, when suddenly, between my conveyers, I noticed a certain movement.

"There's someone here," said one voice in a whisper.

"It's a rolled-up sail," replied another.

"No, there's something alive here," retorted the first.

After a minute's silence, I heard a cry – the rustle of a sliding dagger, and the weak groan of a dying man.

"Stop! Stop!" shouted several voices around us.

This was already too much: I couldn't hold out any longer and tore off the blindfold. The moon was shining – and at my feet there lay a bloodied corpse! I had still not come to my senses at the sight of this horrible spectacle, when the boat on which I found myself was attached by hooks to another one, out from which at the same moment jumped unknown people, from whose uniforms I guessed had to be police operatives. My conveyers were already no longer in the boat. Several shots, coming from soldiers, forced me to conclude that my previous acquaintances had thrown themselves into the sea.

My new acquaintances didn't leave me a minute for reflection, didn't allow me to say as much as a word, and without ceremony tied my hands and put me into a police barge. To my question, as to where they were taking me, one of the assembled replied: "To the place where we usually take bold young fellows like you!"

There was no reassurance for me in this reply. To everything I said, to any evidence that I knew nothing about these goings-on, they replied that this was not their business and that tomorrow everything would be looked into properly.

The boat was moored to the shore. We got out and, having walked not very far along some or other side streets, we stopped in front of a large building beside which stood sentries. Huge iron doors were turning back on their workings in front of me, but I had hardly been led up to them, when someone, I know not how, shoved a scrap of paper into my hand. I automatically compressed it in my hand and carried on following my escorts, thinking I would finally meet someone with whom I could have things out; but my expectation was in vain. My escorts turned in to a small corridor, opened a small, low door, pushed me through it, and the door slammed – behind me, several doors were locked. Useless would have been any of my shouts: I decided to await patiently the outcome of my lot. I looked around me: it was a small, four-cornered room, without a bed, without a chair, even without windows. A small opening, about four metres from the floor, with an iron grille, let light into the room from a lantern situated outside. When all around me reigned a complete silence, interrupted at times by the steps of a guard, and occasional groans, seeming to come from neighbouring rooms, I decided to go over to the lit-up circle produced by the reflection from the dim lantern. I unwrapped the note and with difficulty made out from it the following words: "Do not forget the promise you gave and stay calm."

I must confess that this note did little to cheer me up. I saw in it only the weird chain which was tying me to the bloody secret; the second bit of the message I had little trust in.

And I was miserable, and angry, and cold. I could not even walk about in my Italian accommodation: the floor was laid with plate; I constantly slipped from the damp that was on it. The suffocating air caught my breath, the damp penetrated my limbs, and a cold sweat poured from me in a torrent.

All resolve left me. In despair I leant against the wall, which was covered in mould, and bitter reflections were agitating away at my inner self.

So this is human fate! – I thought. And the obstacles I had to overcome to make this trip? For several years on end I had worked away, put by my money, denied myself everything to save up a modest sum – all so as to see Italy. That was the thought I would go to bed with and wake up with. Finally I achieved my desired goal, leaving my homeland, my relatives and friends, everything dear to my heart... And what for? So as to all but lose my life, to experience every possible disparagement on the part of some good-for-nothings or other, and, turning away from a cut finger, to see at my feet a man swimming in blood, and, in conclusion, to land in prison and be all but charged with a criminal offence – and to spend my first night in Italy on a bare floor under a moulded-up vault... And who knew what else awaited me? My thoughts were becoming all the gloomier from one hour to the next. I now understood defenders of the corrective system, who advise locking a criminal in a dark room and removing him from all human contact. Nothing submerges a man into himself, nothing moves him into a world of abstract notions, in the same way as loneliness, darkness and silence. I, a cheerful, happy-go-lucky inhabitant of a capital city, for whom the renting of a flat had been the height of abstraction in my life of ideas: I had suddenly been turned into a philosopher and had unexpectedly arrived at the most important questions in human life – any occupation with which until now had seemed to me empty pedantry, or reveries leading to nothing.

Soon fatigue, and the monotonous steps of the guard, plunged me into the land of nod. My thoughts, with every passing hour, got more and more muddled, joining up with half-dreams. Cold hands were grabbing me by the shoulders; or an icy mass was crawling down my cheeks; or lifeless leaden faces would appear – and from their eyes, over blue furrows rolled tears of blood, dropping down and winding around me in a web. Then I thought I was attached to the pendulum of a huge clock and at every stroke I was hopelessly trying to cling to the slippery wall. I was constantly waking up and falling asleep.

I don't know how long I remained in this condition. When I came to, I was very surprised that the guard's steps, the only sign of life amid this horrific silence, had ceased. Probably, it was this same circumstance that made me wake up. But my surprise increased all the more when I felt the wall behind me moving. At first I thought it was a fantasy of my disturbed imagination; but, having half risen, I saw clearly the bricks in the wall actually shifting. An involuntary impulse forced me to touch them. I very gently pulled one of them out; and hardly had I pulled it when an iron bar appeared in the opening. An unknown voice whispered to me in Italian: "Russian, Russian." Half-asleep, and not being in a state to render account of my thoughts, I, by unwitting movement and by a genuinely strong desire to get out of my dungeon, grabbed hold of the bar and began to bring down the rest of the bricks. But, at that very minute, the doors of my dungeon banged open, a shout resounded from the opening, shots were to be heard and alarm raised. I found myself surrounded by jailers. At this point, there was nothing I could say: the iron bar was in my hands! The desire to run was manifest!... And I, my strength totally collapsing, allowed myself to be tied up, without saying a word. From this room they took me to another, even worse than the first one: this one was barely two metres in length and width.

They threw me onto a tuft of rotten straw and riveted me to a chain fixed to the wall. This room had no opening apart from a small slit in the door, into which the guard's face was constantly being stuck. I spent several hours in this awful state. The idea that I had given myself the appearance of a criminal in flight, and the uncomfortable position in which I found myself, did not allow me to relax my eyes for a single minute. Eventually I noticed some sort of a whitish light in the opening of the door, due to which I guessed that morning had come.

This light was a great comfort to me. However things may end up, I thought, at least I'll get out of this tortuous position! And, indeed, after a little while some noise was heard, the door opened, the incoming keepers unlocked the belt pinning me to the wall and, surrounding me with unsheathed swords, led me out from my compact lodging. We walked along several corridors and found ourselves in the inner yard of the prison fortress. The sun was coming up, a light breeze fanned me with warm air, and I appreciated that feeling that people have when they emerge from lengthy confinement to the bright sky.

Soon my escorts led me into a room in which scribes were sitting behind tables. We walked past them; they barely raised their heads – probably such scenes were quite customary for them. Eventually my escorts brought me into a room, where there sat behind a large table a man in a black tailcoat, rather stout, who, screwing up his little eyes, asked me my name. I told him my name and added that I found myself in such a strange situation, which I could explain only to the Russian envoy. At that instant, my new acquaintance sent a clerk for my papers and then, turning to me, said:

"Your wish to see the Russian envoy will be granted, provided, of course, that he will agree to your request. But I must forewarn you that, if you are indeed that person whom you make yourself out to be, then your envoy will not have the right, and even will not wish, to interfere in a case of murder. In any event, you will be judged according to the laws of the land in which you find yourself, and no one on earth will be in a position to save you from the fate that awaits a murderer. Only your voluntary confession and the naming of your accomplices can slightly soften the severity of the law."

"Murder?" I yelled. "Accomplices? But, in the name of God, who am I supposed to have killed?"

"You will be aware that you were caught over the corpse of a police operative who had been assigned to the observation of a crime in preparation."

"My dear sir!" I replied, "I couldn't kill anyone, because I myself was a prisoner on that same boat, the one the police found me on."

"A prisoner? But what evidence do you have for that?"

"The fact, my dear sir, that I was sitting in the boat with my eyes bound up."

The official picked up a piece of cloth lying on the table, which I recognized as my earlier blindfold. He held it against my face, trying to keep to the impressions that remained on it, and indeed could see that it did fit me.

"This evidence, it is true, somewhat serves as corroboration for what you have said; but why and through what means did you come to be on that boat?"

"That is something I cannot tell you. I have given the solemn vow of a man of honour not to reveal this secret to anyone."

"You may judge for yourself," the official said to me, "that this circumstance serves to increase judicial suspicion, all the more so as an attempt was made this night to free you. This could not have been made without your agreement – which, there again, complements further the situation in which you were caught."

I tried to explain, as well as I could, that I had no notion about the people who wanted to free me. I tried to explain that involuntary urge, which at the instant of my awakening from my sleep, had compelled me, against my own will, to assist my unknown liberators. But I myself felt that everything I said was just obscure. Meanwhile, my papers were brought in; having taken a look at them, the official said to me:

"Indeed, from your papers I can see that you are a foreigner, who only yesterday evening arrived in Naples, and that it would be improbable to suppose you the murderer of an unknown police operative. But, you will agree yourself, that the circumstances of your case are extremely strange: the commission will not be in a position to discharge you, if you do not provide the necessary explanations. Write a letter to your envoy: perhaps he will convince you to be more forthcoming."

I thanked the official for his concern towards me and hurried to write the letter. When I had finished it, the official said to me:

"Your letter will be sent immediately. While awaiting a reply, you will excuse us, if we have to observe the precautionary measures that are usually taken in such cases."

They led me into my previous room, but no longer put the chains on me.

Within a few minutes, I received permission to appear before the envoy, though in the company of a gendarme. The envoy received me in the best way he could and, already having news of me both from letters and from what my fellow passengers from the boat had said, he got himself fully into my situation. He understood the sense of honour that forbade me to reveal the whole secret. However, he told me that all he could do on my behalf was to certify before the Neapolitan government as to my rank and conduct. He added that everything further he would have to leave to the rulings of their national judicial court.

All this, I confess, did little to console me, especially when, on going out from the envoy, I was invited by the gendarme officer into our previous carriage. The devil take it! – I thought – I came to Naples for a purpose. A wonderful treatment, walking for the good of my health beneath unsheathed swords and breathing the mouldy air of prison fortresses! On returning to my unfortunate accommodation, I was taken into a room that was somewhat better than the previous one. This time all precautions were confined to just my word of honour that I would undertake nothing untoward before my lot was decided. In that state I passed the day until evening, and only the setting of the sun reminded me that for more than a day I had had nothing in my stomach: thus can a strong emotional disturbance awaken physical needs in a person! But hardly had I realized this, when at the same instant I was feeling the most severe hunger, and the few pieces of macaroni brought in by the scruffy keeper seemed to me the tastiest dish that had ever befallen me in my entire life. Such was my first dinner in Naples. I had not yet managed to finish up this mean feast, when once again the police officer came in to see me.

"Your envoy," he said, "has taken you under his guarantee of bail. From now on you are free, but please be so kind first to confirm by signature your verbal deposition given before the official this morning, and equally to sign your undertaking to appear before the court at the first summons."

I signed everything they wanted me to and, beside myself with joy, leaped out from the place of my detention. I no longer wished to stay in that inn which had been the cause of my unhappy adventure, and that same day I transported, or more accurately carried, my bag to another one, *alla Vittoria*, right by the gates of the charming *Villa Reale*. I had no time to rest, before the innkeeper came in to hand me a package.

"From whom is this?" – I asked.

"I don't know," – he replied.

I must confess that I unwrapped this package with great displeasure, so alarmed was I by any mystery at all.

In the package was to be found a ring of ancient workman-ship, on which were embossed some sort of, what seemed to me like Egyptian figures – a snake with a lion's head, some kind of vessel, and signs and letters incomprehensible to me. With the ring was a note:

"You, without knowing it, have saved the life of a certain person. People who are indebted to you did not dare to insult you with a monetary payment. But they hope you will not refuse to accept, as a memento of this, the ring here enclosed. It may some day stand you in good stead. Besides, as you may see for yourself, this ring belongs to the number of such rarities valued by your countrymen and which cannot be obtained for money. However, for some time to come, you will do well not to show it to anyone. We regret once again disturbing your tranquillity."

With little knowledge of antiquities, I scarcely paid attention to the marvellous ring and nearly threw it out of the window – as just the thought of anything connected with my adventure turned me cold. However, after slight reflection I placed the ring in my shaving box.

I spent several days in complete solitude awaiting a fresh visit from the police official, but he did not appear. I don't know whether entreaties made by the envoy, or the intrigues of my unknown enemy-friends were the reason for me being left in peace. Eventually I cheered up. The magazines brought to me by my innkeeper talked about a new singer who had brought delight to the whole of Naples. I decided to go off to San Carlo. Coming down the staircase of the inn I noticed a little old man, heavily powdered, who had come down from above, in a black tailcoat. There was some sort of a strange agitation about his whole person. Negotiating the stairs, his whole being would move: his hands, his nose, his eyes – all were in some kind of motion. Looking at him, one could think that something or other once in his life had shocked him, and had frozen him for evermore in this condition. All these observations I registered only subsequently, as at that precise minute I glanced at him with that indifferent curiosity with which you look at some neighbour, for, from his conversation on encountering the innkeeper, I gathered that my old man was living in the same building with me. Not wishing to make a new acquaintance, I went on my way. Having walked down several streets, I turned round and, to my extreme astonishment, I saw that my old man was following me. Frightened by everything that had happened to me, I was very displeased with this accompaniment. Wishing to dispense with my companion, I went up to the first person I encountered and asked him to show me the nearest way to San Carlo. At this moment the little old man caught up with me and, hearing my question, said with great haste: "You're going to San Carlo? You must be a foreigner? You don't know the way? I am going exactly there... would you care to walk with me?"

To refuse was impossible. Continuing on the way, my old man talked ceaselessly. He threw questions at me, not waiting for answers. He managed to tell me that he was a great lover of antiquities, had a big collection of coins, and was living in the same establishment as me. He also said that at the theatre would be performing a singer who had for a long time not appeared on stage; that it must be very cold in Russia; that the food in our inn was not always good; that Signora Grandini had two or three false notes in her voice; and that he himself cooked wonderful pasta...

All this was wonderfully mixed up within the conversation of Sig. Ambrosio Benevolo – such being the name of my new acquaintance.

We went into the theatre and took up two free places together. They were presenting Donizetti's *Anna Bolena*. Struck by the magnificence of the spectacle, I didn't take my eyes from it. But imagine my astonishment when I recognized, in the prima donna, the woman whom I had seen on the first night of my stay in Naples. I didn't know what I was to do: in any case, to walk out would have been ridiculous, and could only have aroused the suspicion of my pursuers. Meanwhile, my companion was out of his senses with delight. All the singer's roulades he repeated with his whole body and, before a cadenza, he lowered his boots little by little, folded his arms, held his breath, shivered as though in a fever, and at the end of a trill, in a total frenzy, jumped from his seat bootless, yelled out several interjections and clapped his hands for all he was worth. During the recitative he would quieten down and again very coolly would turn to me with questions: do they wear a lot of fur coats in Russia? Do I have a collection of medals? How do I like my *frutti di mare*? But hardly had the prima donna started a new aria, than Benevolo would be again beside himself, slipping off his boots and clapping his hands. At any other time, I, a cold northern resident, would have been highly amused by this transformation, all the more so as I could see similar convulsive movements going on in many other parts of the hall. But right now I was very distracted by my strange encounter with the prima donna. I was wrestling within myself – between the desire to ask my new acquaintance something about her, and the fear that this would be an infringement of my vow. It even seemed to me as though the prima donna had recognized me, and that her eyes were often involuntarily turning in my direction. I hardly dared to look at her: the court scene with its sepulchral music reminded me so vividly of my adventures that I almost choked.

Benevolo was looking at me from under his eyebrows; however, he didn't say a word. I could not know for sure whether he had noticed my discomfort or not. Despite all that, an involuntary feeling was drawing me to Signora Grandini: she had a wonderful stage presence. Several sharp features on her face were softened by the distance; in her voice there was something penetrating, something touching – it was not completely pure and clear, but sonorous yet soft, as though coated with velvet. However, I must confess that I was very glad when the curtain came down.

The next day, when I awoke, I spotted on my table a note, but one written in a hand new to me:

"People who wish you well do not advise you to go to the Teatro di San Carlo."

I confess that this did exasperate me: I saw myself tied into an intrigue, which affixed a chain to all my actions and from which there was no way I could free myself. That day I decided to leave Naples. I was still reflecting on my plans, when at my door I heard someone singing in a quivering voice: "*Cerca un lido, dove sicuro...*"* The door opened: and it was Benevolo. He straight away jumped on me with his questions. How had I spent the night? How did I like the Teatro di San Carlo? Did I drink chocolate? What did I think of Donizetti, of Bellini? And his questions were intermingled with exclamations – *stupendo, stupenda!* – it was impossible to guess what these referred to: to the music, to Donizetti, to Bellini, or to chocolate.

I could not manage replies to his questions, for Ambrosio didn't wait for an answer. He brought me a whole pile of coins and medals, showing me each one separately, carried away by each of them, and suggested to me an exchange for Russian money, whatever I happened to have. This was a skilful invitation to buy from him some of his rarities. In order to get rid of the importunate old fellow, I exchanged a few Russian ten-rouble notes, which I had on me, for his rarities and hastened to set off for the envoy's, for my passport and other papers. At the embassy, they told me that, before giving me my passport, the Ambassador without fail would have to communicate with the Neapolitan government: this would be bound to delay my departure for a few days.

After that I didn't go out any more anywhere. Benevolo did not forget to visit me; every day he would bring me, as before, medals and cameos, amusing me by taking from them copies with the greatest dexterity. Once he brought me a greened over and almost faded Russian rouble and spoke much, and for ages, about its antiquity, about his guesses as to how, over three hundred years before, it could have been brought to Italy. I interrupted his disquisition with the remark that three hundred years ago round coins had not existed in Russia. This remark somewhat took the wind out of his sails. Another time he brought me several bags of various medals and asked me if he could leave them in my room for a while, saying that he had his suspicions about a few lovers of antiquities who wanted to rob him of his treasure, but who surely would not come looking for them in my room – all the more so as I don't go out anywhere. I allowed him to do as he pleased, just so as to get shot of him.

Finally, to my immense satisfaction, I received news from one of my associates who worked at the embassy that I could get my passport the next day. I didn't want to delay for a minute, so I hired a coachman and got down to packing my modest wardrobe. Benevolo caught me at this task: "You're packing already! Where are you going? Probably to Rome? Don't forget to stop off in Milan at the Ambrosian Library, there's splendid food at the *Albergo Reale* inn," and so on, and so on. I carried on with my task, answering the old man just with interjections. I don't know how, but sorting through my shaving box, I dropped my mystery ring. It rolled on the floor; I bent over and collided with Benevolo, who was also sticking his hand out after the ring, and when I, not displaying my rarity, clasped it between my fingers, Benevolo turned pale. For as long as I live, I shall not forget his figure at that moment. He moved in a total shake, his elbows rooted to his sides, while waving both his hands, raising first one leg and then the other, opening his mouth wide, blinking his eyes and stretching out his neck.

"Sell that ring to me," he said, gasping away at me.

"No, I won't sell it," I replied.

"Allow me at least to make a copy of it."

"I can't do that, either."

"At least, show it to me."

"I can't do that, either. Make a journey to me in Russia for it, and then, perhaps, I might even give it to you."

"To Russia, to Russia!" said Benevolo, "that's impossible. But why can't you even show it to me here? Is there really some secret attached to your ring?"

"Yes, a secret," I replied.

"A nice secret, too!" Benevolo yelled. "Do you want me to tell you what is depicted on your ring? It has on it a vessel, a snake with a lion's head, a mummy with a bird's nose, and the name 'Ioa' round it – isn't that right?"

"Perhaps; but, all the same, I can't show you the ring."

"This is strange!" said Benevolo, hopping around the room, "very strange! It's really extraordinary how strange it is!... So, you don't want to hand me the ring?" he said after a short silence.

"I can't," I replied, with considerable annoyance.

"You definitely don't want to?"

"Definitely."

"No, tell me truthfully! You really cannot in any way show me the ring?"

I turned away from him in silence.

The obsessive old fellow took this as a sign of indecision: he rushed at me from the other side, propped his elbows against his sides and muttered at me with an air of utter servility:

"It seems, then, that it is possible for you to show me the ring."

"You are making me lose all patience," I said to him finally in a threatening voice and stamped my foot.

Benevolo took a few jumps around the room, went out, and did not come back to see me again.

In the evening, when I had gone to bed in the sweet hope of finally leaving this, for me, city of ill fortune, the innkeeper again appeared to me with a note.

"What is it now?" I asked in anger. "Who gave you this note?"

"Someone I don't know," he answered.

The content of the note was fully sufficient to arouse my anger; it contained just the following words:

"Your friends advise you, if you value your life, not to leave Naples for some time to come."

I cursed my friends from the bottom of my heart. At first I thought this was a joke from Benevolo. However, the handwriting was the same as on that note which I had received before my acquaintance with him. Nevertheless, despite everything, I decided that, come what may, I would travel out of Naples, and even out of Italy, which had now become repulsive to me.

On the next day, I hurried off for my passport, but had hardly entered the Ambassador's offices, when I was called into his bureau. The Ambassador received me with such an expression that I was seriously frightened.

"To my extreme regret," he said, "I cannot give you back your passport. The opposite is the case: I have to invite you to appear before the court of this place. Your business has become entangled in new circumstances. It is all so strange that I cannot believe your participation in it, and at the same time it's so consequential that I cannot refuse the local government. You may already be aware that one of the singers of the opera theatre here, Eulalia Grandini, has disappeared without trace. She was greatly loved by the public of this place and the general alarm concerning her fate forces the police to adopt the strictest measures."

"I have been out of the inn so little that this is the first I have even heard of it."

"However, at your place has been seen a ring, or a band, belonging to this artiste," the Ambassador told me, directing upon me a piercing gaze.

I became unwittingly confused; however, pulling myself together, I decided to reveal to the Ambassador that part of the secret, to the preservation of which I was not obligated by my word of honour.

"Indeed," I said, "I did receive some ring, but I do not know from whom."

"With some mystical signs or other, and the inscription 'Ioa'?" asked the Ambassador.

"Exactly," I replied.

"That's very strange. From these papers, I see that this ring used to belong to some secret society or other, who valued it very highly, and whose members are now undergoing prosecution by the government."

I explained to the Ambassador the way in which this ring fell to me.

"Indeed," he said to me, "the government here presupposes some sort of a connection between this circumstance and the abduction of Grandini, as well as with the killing of a police officer. As if that were not enough," continued the Ambassador, "you are accused of having links with a certain Ambrosio Benevolo, who is suspected of the forging of false coinage."

My arms sank.

"I am sure," continued the Ambassador, that you will justify yourself on the charges levelled against you, but my duty forces me to give you over to the Neapolitan government. Do not reproach me for that. Put yourself in my position: you would do the same thing. I have a moral belief in your innocence, but, thanks to your reticence, no legal confidence at all."

I thanked the Ambassador for his truly paternal concern for me, but firmly repeated that I would rather undergo every possible unpleasantness than betray my solemnly given word of honour.

The Ambassador, as I have said already, was a decent person; he understood me completely, promised to do everything on his part to extract me from my unfortunate situation and then... he again offered me the companionship of an officer of the gendarmes.

I shall not bore you any further with the tale of my discussions with the officials who questioned me: it would be a repetition of almost all those particulars of which you are already aware. I shall add only that all this questioning did not in the least provide me with an explication of my secret.

One thing was clear – that they wanted nothing to come of the case. All the questions put to me were as though just ready-made, indeterminate, superficial, at times strange to a point of improbability. I was asked about all the trivialities of my private life: at what time did I get up, what did I do in the morning, what in the evening, whether I know the ancient languages, whether I can draw... From all this, however, I did understand that Benevolo was their informant on me: but how had he himself landed in with the prosecution? Meanwhile, more than three weeks went past. Every day I steadied myself for something decisive and, finally, to my inexpressible pleasure and surprise, they announced to me that I was free. They returned to me my things, which had been taken from me for the duration of the proceedings, with the exception of the ring. I regretted this but little and, what was most pleasing to me of all, I finally received permission to leave Naples.

After that, I travelled around Italy for almost a year, completely peacefully, and eventually, amid the distracted life of the traveller, had almost forgotten my Neapolitan adventure.

On one occasion in Venice, at a ball at Countess Graziana's, I caught sight of a woman in a blue dress, who flashed past me in another contra-dance group. Her face seemed to me to be familiar: I enquired her name of the lady dancing with me. Such precautions are essential to the travelling man: you meet so many people, who appear and disappear before your eyes, that there is always the risk of starting to speak to a lady you don't know, and of going straight past one whose house you have been in.

"Oh, that's the renowned Countess Lucchensini!"

"Renowned? Why is that?" I asked.

"She is a woman of some character," she replied. "Beware of falling into her nets. She managed to get married to her teacher at the age of fifteen; meanwhile promising her hand to another young man; and for a period of six years concealing her matrimony. She was able to deceive her guardian; and eventually to divorce her husband and marry another – and still bear her husband's name."

"But how is that?" I asked my lady. "Was her teacher really Count Lucchensini?"

"Yes, exactly," the lady replied. "Count Lucchensini was the son of that Lucchensini who, as perhaps you have heard, perished on the scaffold; the estate was confiscated and the son was forced to take up giving lessons."

"One cannot, however, blame the poor Countess," broke in another lady, who had been listening to our conversation. "Her mother was a woman of a strange disposition, who became all the more unbearable from her ceaseless illness. Right up to her death, the poor Countess was forced to live as a complete recluse. The only people she met were her teachers. Is it any wonder that she would fall for one of them, who was young, handsome, and who was able to introduce all the disappointments of a man of society into the close relations between a teacher and his pupil? He fell in love with her, and she with him. But as her mother would never have agreed to a match between her and such a man, then is it any surprise that she decided to marry him in secret?"

The contra-dance concluded. I exchanged bows with my lady and involuntarily turned my eyes on the Countess, so as to recollect of whom she reminded me. Besides, a man's glance always unwittingly pauses on a woman possessing sufficient firmness of spirit to despise the opinion of society: she arouses curiosity, mixed with a certain type of involuntary respect. One's mind unwittingly thinks of the struggle that this woman must have endured with herself and with all those around her, and one's heart can imagine the sufferings she would have had to bear, in order to escape from other, even more severe, sufferings.

All these thoughts were crowding through my head when I looked at the Countess, and it seemed to me that I had attracted her attention to myself. And indeed, she also began to scrutinize me and, as I was walking past her, she said to me: "*Signore!*"...

I stopped in my tracks: her voice startled me.

"It seems you do not recognize me?" she went on.

I stepped back a pace, for it seemed to me that before me stood Signora Grandini. The moments of agitation in which I saw her, together with her hairdo – at that time ladies were only beginning to wear their hair up – had prevented me from recognizing her in the first instant.

"I don't know," I said, "whether I should recognize you."

"Oh, don't worry!" the Countess answered me with a smile. "Those who imposed that awful oath on you don't really exist any more. I have the full right to release you from all your vows. If you want to know more, then call on me tomorrow evening. You ought to be rewarded for that humiliating situation which you found yourself in, through my graces. By the way," she continued, "tell me, did my ring stand you in good stead?"

"Your ring? The one with the mystical signs? It remained in the hands of the Neapolitan government."

"Really, then that good-for-nothing Benevolo profited through it!"

"So, you knew Benevolo?"

"Benevolo?" she repeated with a smile. "Tomorrow everything will be explained to you."

The next day, at the appointed hour, I hurried to Countess Lucchensini's and, in the first place, I was very taken aback when the commissionaire told me that the Countess was not receiving. However, when I mentioned my name, he immediately rang a bell and the doors opened in front of me. I passed through a series of magnificent rooms, luxuriously decorated with taste. The Countess was waiting for me in a pavilion situated at the end of the house, the balcony of which gave out on one side on to the Grand Canal and on the other to an empty square. She was seated on a divan, in a light muslin dress, surrounded by flowering oranges, and she indicated to me the seat beside her.

"You have to know that you are my deliverer," she said.

"Your deliverer?" I repeated.

"Yes. But for you, I would quite possibly have had to bid farewell to life. You, without even knowing it yourself, untied the knot in my existence. I think that you have already been told my story before. Everyone relates the whole thing with various ridiculous additions. I am not going to justify myself before you. I shall tell you just one thing: there was no way I couldn't marry Lucchensini, because I was being persecuted by that same Benevolo, the one whom you know. Exploiting the illness of my mother, living in our house, where he occupied the post first of teacher and then of major-domo, Ambrosio never gave me a minute's peace. Lucchensini was young and handsome. Benevolo was almost always the same as you have seen him. I preferred the former.

"It takes a long time to tell you my story. Suspicion fell on my clandestine husband, the reason for which being his father's connections. Wanting to open a certain path for himself, after the marriage he went off to seek his fortune in Russia. In his place there came to me a new admirer: my distant relative, Leonardo Amati. You will have been told, I am sure, that I promised to marry him. That is true, but this is how it happened. With the help of his cunning father and my mother's confessor, he was able to drive Mother, who was physically and morally distraught, to demand of me, in her last breath, that I should marry Leonardo. In that moment of grief I promised her everything; Mummy passed away and, in the will she left, she nominated Vincenzo Amati, Leonardo's father, as guardian over me and over all my huge estate. After the initial grief, which Mummy's passing produced in me, Leonardo began reminding me of my promise. I declared firmly that I was already married. This revelation infuriated Leonardo and his father, who had hoped by means of this match to get hold of my estate for evermore. They used all possible means to force me to dissolve my marriage to Lucchensini. Gifted by nature with a resolute character, I ran away from Venice, changed my name, and Signora Grandini appeared in various theatres of Italy, to rousing applause and surrounded by a crowd of admirers. The large fees received through my talent provided me with the means to put a stop to all the machinations of Amati for the annulment of my marriage.

"Meanwhile my way of life was so much to my liking that I had soon forgotten my husband; and he too, it seems, forgot about me. My guardian, after futile searches, finally found me in Naples. I had not yet then come of age and my guardian still had full authority over me. He obtained false evidence of my husband's demise and insistently demanded the fulfilment of my promise. I knew that this was untrue, since almost at the same time I had received a letter from the Count, in which he informed me that he had finally been able to persuade the government of his innocence and that he was returning to Italy. I pretended to believe my persecutors, adorned myself in a black widow's dress and allowed my room to be covered in black cloth – only so as to gain time, since not very long remained before my coming of age. But the cunning Amati guessed my pretence and found out at the same time that Lucchensini was on the first ship due to get in to Naples. For Amati, this was a decisive moment. He saw that I was giving him the slip, but did not want to have me triumph without some vengeance. Perhaps he hoped that with my husband's death I would be more gracious to him. Perhaps he also wanted to frighten us both and give us the choice – between death and marriage to Leonardo. I could never understand his intentions very well: perhaps it was simply the impulse of his wild Calabrian character. You know the means he used for the attainment of his goal. The remote house in which we lived, the servants bought off – everything seemingly had to be conducive, yet providence furnished you as the means for the destruction of this design. When, after our encounter, he took you away with him, I decided that, whatever it may cost, I would get myself out of the power of my tormentors. Since my estate was the main reason for their persecution, I took advantage of old Amati's confusion and offered him as a kind of ransom the whole of my estate. He agreed without difficulty. There remained but two days to my coming of age, and I attached my pre-dated signature to a paper in which, having expressed gratitude to Amati for the excellent management of my estate, I declared myself in debt to him for a considerable sum of money. Meanwhile Leonardo returned in tattered clothing, soaked through and in great agitation. He agreed to it all. I then noticed something strange about him, but could not yet find out what had happened to him, because at that very minute I had to leave them to appear again on stage. Only subsequently, when the rumour spread about the killing of a police official, did the thought enter my head that Leonardo must have taken part in this incident. Indeed, a month later, one of his servants told the authorities everything. Leonardo perished on the scaffold and his father died from despair. The police operative had fallen into this adventure by accident. In our area there had been various thefts. Noticing something suspicious in Leonardo's boat, the police official, carried away by fervour for his profession, decided to conceal himself under the sail, to try to discover something definite. All this I learned subsequently, when rumours reached me of Leonardo's arrest. Having nothing to live on, I again took to the theatre in Naples, under the name of Grandini."

The Countess stopped for a bit.

"I have told you," she then went on, "everything that you might be curious about in my story. I will add only that my estate was returned to me. The Count and I met up again and we both noted such an indifference, one to the other, that without any argument we decided to separate. He is now petitioning in Rome for the annulment of our marriage."

"Thank you very much, Countess; but for me there is still one unintelligible figure in your story – Benevolo."

"Benevolo!" – the Countess repeated the name, adopting a significant air. "I can't tell you anything in that regard at this moment. If you want to find out something about him, then you must go out of my house, going through all the rooms, sit in the boat, return here by this side-street and come up to me by this balcony: a ladder will be lowered for you."

I was in two minds about this; but the Countess so smiled at me, and gave me her hand with such an air, that I could not refuse her.

I carried out to the letter all her instructions. But, I have to confess, my heart missed a beat when I began to clamber up the rope ladder, which was lowered for me from the balcony. I found the Countess in the same light dress; she greeted me with a smile and indicated to me the door of a small chamber. Going into it, I saw all the accessories of male night-time attire and lost no time in putting them to good use. When I looked out from the door, the Countess started laughing and indicated to me the place on the divan beside her, rang the bell, and placed on the table a brace of pistols.

"What does this mean?" I asked her.

"These are essential," the Countess told me in a significant tone.

I pondered all this and unwittingly looked over the cocking pieces of the two pistols.

The door opened, and Benevolo rushed into the room.

"Ambrosio!" the Countess said to him, "are you acquainted with this young man?"

Benevolo trembled with his whole body.

"You see, Ambrosio, I left one husband, refused another, and here is my third – and still it's not you! Poor Ambrosio! But now that's not the point: you are aware of everything that you have done to this young man. He is asking me for vengeance. Your last minute has come: – make your confession. Interrogate him, Count!" she said, turning to me.

I could not look at Benevolo without laughing, but at the same time he did arouse in me an instinctive pity.

The Countess sensed that feeling in me and said:

"Oh, how good you are, Count – you still feel sorry for him! You don't know the sort of man he is! That he should have dared to fall in love with me, that's the least of it! Oh, yes! Maddened by his failure, he went over to the side of my enemies. He helped Amati; he was dispatched by them to you – as a spy; he wrote those notes to you; he prevented you from seeing me, for Leonardo was afraid that our meeting would reveal his crime. And that's little enough. When he found out that my ring was in your possession, the one he had been trying to get hold of for ages, he decided to bring against you the absurd denunciation of my abduction, in order to be able to profit from this rarity amidst the judicial intrigues... Of course, you do know that he is a lover of antiquities?"

"He seems to me," I remarked, "more a lover of money than of antiquities: he was himself held for the making of forged money."

"Oh, no!" said the Countess. "He wouldn't have enough spirit for that. It's true, he has made false coins, though not new ones, but ancient ones. He indulged himself in the most virginal of handicrafts – he invented imaginary monarchs, or made imitations of rare medallions, and drove antiquarians to despair."

Ambrosio trembled with his whole body and just occasionally came out with:

"*Pregiatissima signora*!... *Signor conte*!"*

Finally, when the Countess had stopped talking, he exclaimed, with tears in his eyes:

"All that is true, completely true. But, do remember that I saved the Russian Count's life."

"Yes, that is true. Remember the face that looked out from behind the door at our first meeting. For that, it would seem, it might be possible to forgive him, Count. What do you think?"

I was feeling so sorry for poor Ambrosio that I started asking the Countess to bring this joke to an end.

125

"Thank the Count – and then, off you go!" said the Signora, "and tomorrow morning write me a sonnet on this escapade."

Benevolo threw himself at her feet, and then sprang out of the room.

"He is a kind old man," went on the Countess, turning to me, "that is to say, while you keep your hands on him. He's still head over heels in love with me. I am just used to him, like a pet poodle. He never stops drawing silhouettes of me, writes poetry to me and is always beside himself with excitement whenever I allow him to kiss my finger. I wanted, Count, to provide you with this small pleasure, for I would never forgive myself that a noble person should be subjected to insult for my sake and remain unable to get even. If Leonardo were alive, I should without fail have given you a meeting with him; but that, unfortunately, is impossible. Though now your role has terminated. So, farewell!"

"What!" I said to the Countess, "have I to go and get dressed again? And again go down from this balcony on such a dark and rainy night?..."

NOTES

p. 9, *Hoffmann*: E.T.A. Hoffmann, 'Councillor Krespel' (1818), quoted here in J.M. Cohen's translation.

p. 10, *taken Hall's fancy*: Franz Joseph Hall (1758–1828): Austrian founder of phrenology.

p. 12, *my Battle of Waterloo*: Odoevsky (or rather his Beethoven) really means *Wellington's Victory, or the Battle of Victoria* (commonly known as his "Battle Symphony"), performed in Vienna in 1813.

p. 12, *mind what that pedant Weber says*: Jacob Gottfried Weber (1779–1839) – the well-known contrapuntist of our time, who is not to be mistaken for the composer of *Der Freischütz* – strongly and justifiably criticised *Wellington's Victory*, the weakest of Beethoven's compositions, in his fascinating and scholarly journal *Cecilia*. (ODOEVSKY'S NOTE)

p. 13, *my father – Friedrich of blessed memory*: Odoevsky is here making use of a legend, current in the earlier half of the nineteenth century, that Beethoven had been the illegitimate son of Friedrich-Wilhelm II of Prussia (who had stayed in Bonn in 1770).

p. 13, *Es war einmal... grossen Floh*: An early Beethoven song, 'The Song of the Flea', dating from approximately 1789–90.

p. 13, *of which Beethoven had defined Mignon*: Kennst du das Land, etc. ('Knowest thou the land' etc.) (ODOEVSKY'S NOTE).

p. 18, *Opere del Cavaliere Giambattista Piranesi*: "The Works of the Cavalier Giambattista Piranesi": Giovanni

Battista Piranesi (1720–78) was an Italian archaeologist, architect and engraver, specializing in fantastic projects, who came to be much admired in the Europe of Romanticism.

p. 19, *lazzarone*: A beggar boy or pickpocket.

p. 20, *the only leaf in my Elzevir*: Elzevir: the name of a famous Dutch firm of publishers of specially printed books, operating from 1592 until 1712.

p. 20, *the copy had full margins*: "It is well known that for bibliomaniacs the width of margins plays a big role. There is even a special instrument for measuring them, and a few lines more or less often increases or decreases the price of the book by as much as a half." (ODOEVSKY'S NOTE)

p. 20, *generosity, proposes the novels of Genlis*: Genlis, Countess of (1746–1830): French sentimentalist author of society and historical novels (also known as "Madame de Genlis").

p. 21, *with illustrations by Nestor Maximovich Ambodik*: Nestor Maximovich Ambodik-Maximovich (1744–1812): professor of obstetrics and medical author; the popular work here mentioned was published in St Petersburg, 1784–86.

p. 21, *the Bonati Thesaurus medico-practicus undique collectus*: This probably refers to a medical thesaurus published by Bonetus Theophilus (Geneva, 1691).

p. 21, *les villages de Bodegrave et Swammerdam*: The full and correct title of the work is: *Advis fidelle aux véritables Hollandois touchant ce qui s'est passé dans les villages de Bodegrave et Swammerdam, et les cruautés inouies que les François y ont exercées*. In English: "Reliable advice to the staunch Dutch people, concerning what has gone on in the villages of Bodegrave and Swammerdam, and the unprecedented cruelties that the French carried out there" (French).

p. 21, *Hortus sanitatis... par forme de dictionnaire*: "Garden of health" (Latin); "Garden of devotion", "Flowers of eloquence, picked in the cabinets of the rarest spirits to express amorous passions of one sex for the other, in dictionary form" (French).

p. 21, *Virgilius ex recensione Naugerii*: "Virgil in the Naugerii edition" (Latin).

p. 21, *precious Aldine edition*: The Aldine Press was a famous Italian publisher of classical texts in the 15th and 16th centuries.

p. 23, *in The Life of a Gambler*: Vasily Andreyevich Karatygin (1802–53): Russian tragic actor and dramatist, here playing, from 1828, in a popular French drama by Victor Ducange (1783–1833).

p. 24, *he was my teacher*: Michelangelo Buonarroti in fact had lived from 1475 to 1564.

p. 40, *Hastily, he read through Bentham*: Jeremy Bentham (1748–1832), an English thinker much criticised by Odoevsky for his utilitarianism (and stress on 'utility', 'benefit' etc.): see Odoevsky's *Russian Nights* (1844).

p. 40, *he also managed to read Thomson*: James Thomson (1700–48), Scottish nature poet: author of *The Seasons* (1830) and of 'Rule, Britannia'.

p. 40, *a mixture of Bentham, Thomson, Paley*: William Paley (1743–1805), English theological thinker.

p. 40, *Byron*: George Gordon, Lord Byron (1788–1824): the most inspirational English poet for European Romanticism.

p. 41, *Richardson's Clarissa*: *Clarissa, or the History of a Young Lady* (1747–49): the famous English novel by Samuel Richardson (1689–1761).

p. 59, *readers... the Abbot Galiani*: Abbot Ferdinando Galiani (1728–87), Italian thinker and publicist; a leader of "Neapolitan Enlightenment" and an initiator of the Italian utilitarian tradition.

p. 67, *Redgauntlet*: *Redgauntlet* (1824) was one of the Waverley novels of Sir Walter Scott (1771–1832), whose "Scotch novels" were much renowned in Europe.

p. 69, *Irinei Modestovich and I myself*: Irinei Modestovich (surnamed Gomozeyko) would have been familiar to Russian readers of the day, as the tale-gatherer of Odoevsky's cycle *Variegated Tales* (*Pestrye skazki*, 1833). The current story (of 1838), despite further plans, proved to be the garrulous storyteller's only return appearance.

p. 73, *Épître... Discours en vers*: Poetic works by Voltaire (1694–1778), published in the 1730s.

p. 86, *faisait le gros dos*: "Gave himself airs" (French) (ODOEVSKY'S NOTE).

p. 95, *Alle crocelle, a Santa Lucia*: "Tie up near the Santa Lucia" (Italian).

p. 97, *Scellerato*: "Villain" (Italian).

p. 113, *Cerca un lido, dove sicuro*: "I'm searching for a land, where I'll be safe" (Italian).

p. 125, *Pregiatissima signora!... Signor conte*: "Most esteemed Countess!... Sir, the Count!" (Italian).

BIBLIOGRAPHY

ODOEVSKY IN ENGLISH

Odoevsky, Vladimir, *The Salamander and other Gothic Stories,* translated by Neil Cornwell (London: Bristol Classical Press, 1992; and Evanston, IL: Northwestern University Press)

Odoevsky, Vladimir, *Two Princesses*, translated by Neil Cornwell (London: Hesperus, 2010)

Odoevsky, Vladimir, *Russian Nights*, translated by Olga Koshansky-Olienikov and Ralph E. Matlaw (originally, New York: E.P. Dutton, 1965); republished, with an "Afterword" by Neil Cornwell, (Evanston, IL: Northwestern University Press, 1997)

ON ODOEVSKY

Cornwell, Neil, *The Life, Times and Milieu of V.F. Odoyevsky, 1804–1869,* foreword by Sir Isaiah Berlin (London: The Athlone Press/Continuum, 1986; and Athens, OH: Ohio University Press)

Cornwell, Neil, *Vladimir Odoevsky and Romantic Poetics: Collected Essays* (Providence and Oxford: Berghahn Books, 1998)

Cornwell, Neil, ed., *The Society Tale in Russian Literature: from Odoevskii to Tolstoi* (Amsterdam and Atlanta, GA: Rodopi, 1998)

Cornwell, Neil, ed., *The Gothic-Fantastic in Nineteenth-Century Russian Literature* (Amsterdam and Atlanta, GA: Rodopi, 1999)

Cornwell, Neil, *Odoevsky's Four Pathways into Modern Fiction: A Comparative Study* (Manchester: Manchester University Press, 2010)

Sucur, Slobodan, *Poe, Odoyevsky, and Purloined Letters: Questions of Theory and Period Style Analysis* (Frankfurt am Main [etc.]: Peter Lang, 2001)

Whitehead, Claire, *The Fantastic in France and Russia in the Nineteenth Century: In Pursuit of Hesitation* (Oxford: Legenda, 2006)

ACKNOWLEDGEMENTS

Of the translations included here, 'Two Days in the Life of the Terrestrial Globe' and 'The Witness' first appeared as an appendix to my volume *Odoevsky's Four Pathways into Modern Fiction* (see Bibliography). My translation of 'Beethoven's Last Quartet' is already available through the online Literary Encyclopedia (www.litencyc.com).

Kind permission of the publishers, in each case, for reproduction here of these translations is gratefully acknowledged.